I0535204

TEASE ME

THE MACINTYRE BROTHERS BOOK TWO

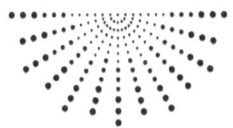

S. E. LUND

ACADIAN PUBLISHING LIMITED

Copyright © 2018 by S. E. Lund

All rights reserved.

No part of this book may be reproduced in any form or by any electronic or mechanical means, including information storage and retrieval systems, without written permission from the author, except for the use of brief quotations in a book review.

❀ Created with Vellum

1

ELLA

I passed the spot where Josh and I first met, and a surge of happiness filled me.

Who would have thought that the first man I literally ran into in Manhattan would be the man I would fall for and would spend my days and nights with? I sure didn't expect it, but as I walked along the sidewalk towards the Macintyre building, I smiled to myself remembering our first encounter. This time, I crossed the street at the crosswalk and went to my favorite coffee shop for my morning cup of java, and when I came back, sure enough, Josh was on his bike, riding up the street -- in the bike lane.

I stopped and waited for him on the sidewalk.

"Fancy meeting you here," I said when he arrived at my side. "Even snow won't stop you from riding that thing."

"I laugh at snow," he said and removed his helmet for a kiss. "We're going to have to stop meeting like this."

I leaned in and pressed my lips against his, smiling the

1

whole time while a zing of desire for him flashed through my body.

"You're the boss," I replied.

"Don't say that," he said and shook his head. "I've recused myself from all matters on the book publishing side of the business now that Rob Kennedy has finally taken over. I'm totally focused on *The Chronicle* and keeping MBC afloat. You won't see me around except maybe once a year when I come by for a board meeting."

I pouted. "No more copier room smooches?"

He laughed. "Well, I can't promise that. I might be tempted to come down for more smooches for you in the copier room or hallways when people are busy. And," he said and slipped his arm around my waist, pulling me closer. "If you accept my invitation to stay with me now and then at my apartment, there will be much much more. Like tonight, for example."

"I'll be happy to accept your invitation."

"You have a standing invitation," he said. "Any night you feel like sleeping in my huge bed, you're welcome."

He kissed me, and this time, it was more passionate. For a moment, I lost myself in him, in the sensation of his lips on mine, his tongue touching mine.

We pulled back and stared into each other's eyes.

"Damn, woman," he said under his breath. "We just got finished less than an hour ago and I already want more."

I smiled coyly. "Sorry, Mr. Macintyre, Sir. I have a job to do."

"You do love to tease me," he said as I deliberately flounced off with a flick of my hair and walked towards the building entrance. I arrived at the front doors with him in tow, his bike at his side.

"I do," I said and blew him a very tiny kiss, just in case any of his other staff or business associates were around. I didn't want to embarrass him. We took the elevator up to Macintyre Publishing's offices and he kissed me once more when the doors opened, and we saw we were alone.

The kiss went on and on, and we got away with no one else riding on the elevator with us until my floor.

"Later," he said and pointed to me. "I need my fix."

"Don't worry," I replied and smiled as the elevator doors closed. "You'll get yours."

I popped my head in to see Sharon on my way to my office. We had a meeting in a half hour and I wanted to make sure it was going forward.

"Good morning," I said. "Are we on for eight thirty?"

She glanced up from her desk and gave me a smile. "We are. Bring your best choices and we'll go over them."

"See you at eight thirty."

I went to my office, which was now starting to look like a person worked there and not a makeshift room with a desk and plastic sheeting. I had a different desk now, with a hutch and ergonomic chair, plus my own filing cabinet and a chair for any visitors. The office was tiny, but it had an actual door and a window, looking out over the building beside ours.

I loved it.

I'd even decorated it with Thanksgiving themed items -- a paper turkey sat on the shelf behind my desk and I had a metallic Happy Thanksgiving sign on one wall. I'd have to take that down to make way for Christmas now that Thanksgiving was officially over.

It would have been hard for me, only a few months ago, to imagine my life the way it was now. I was depressed after my breakup with Jerkface, and I didn't want to stay in Concord, knowing that he was there, working and probably now fucking Bunni on an even more-regular basis. I wanted to escape.

Moving to Manhattan to take an unpaid internship was the best decision I'd made in a very long time.

I spent the next thirty minutes preparing for my meeting with Sharon, but my peace and quiet was shattered by the loud ring of my cell. I had programmed it so that when my father called, an old car horn blared. I knew it was him immediately, and I could prepare mentally for our talks.

"Hi, Dad," I said, wondering why he was calling me at this time in the morning. "To what do I owe this pleasure?"

"Hello, Dear," he replied, his voice sounding distracted. "Your mother and I are making a trip to Manhattan this weekend and will be staying for most of the coming week. Something came up and I have some business to attend to. She wanted to spend some time with you while I'm otherwise occupied."

"That's great," I said, even though I'd seen them the previous week for Thanksgiving. "Where are you guys staying?"

"The Ritz downtown. Your mother wanted to be close to your apartment so you two could do some sightseeing. I'll be in meetings the entire weekend."

"What's up?"

"Just some party business before the new session. I know you aren't interested in politics, so I'll just say it's party business and leave it at that."

"Upcoming by-election?"

"Something like that. Sudden death of an old friend and colleague."

"Oh, I'm sorry, Dad. Who was it?"

"Just a former member of the State legislature when I was a member. We've got to find the right person for the seat and so will be meeting all weekend to strategize."

I made a huge and very audible yawn and then a very loud snore for his benefit and he laughed out loud.

"See, I told you that you wouldn't be interested."

"Right now, I'm reading thriller manuscripts and I'm focused on things that are a bit more exciting than by-elections. Politics is not my thing."

"I know that only too well. I won't bore you with the details, but I know your mother would love to do some early Christmas shopping and you two go to a spa and have the full treatment, maybe go for a nice lunch or two. Whatever it is you two do when you get together."

"I'll be glad to see you both."

"So, what's new with you? Any good books? Are you writing? Have you met any decent young men?"

I laughed at his peppered questions. "Dad, I just spent the long weekend with you and Mom," I said. "I already told you that I've got new friends at work and I'm super busy reading manuscripts. I'm really happy to be living here."

"I know. I just wanted to give you a chance to come clean in case you were actually lonely and wanted to move back."

"Not on your life," I said with a laugh, knowing he was only half-teasing me. "I love it here."

"I know your mother misses having you in Concord, but she wants you to be happy, so I'm glad you are. I'll call you when we arrive. Maybe you can meet us for supper tomorrow."

"Do you want me to meet you at the airport?"

"That's not necessary," he replied. "We're getting in during the day, so you'll be at work. We'll call you with a time for dinner."

"Sounds good. Love you Dad," I said.

"Love you back, Punkin," he replied, using his pet name for me.

I hung up and leaned back, smiling to myself. I was glad to see them, but at the same time, I hoped they didn't take up all my time on the weekend. Josh and I spent the Thanksgiving weekend apart and we wanted to make up for lost time. We were having so much fun with each other, spending our weekends together, that I didn't want to deprive myself.

Still, it would be nice to see them both again. I could take my mom to some of the places I'd grown to love visiting and of course, seeing my dad when he was through with his political meetings.

I SPENT THE REST OF THE DAY FOCUSED ON MY WORK, AND of course, received quite a few texts from Josh.

JOSH: *I already miss the photocopier room...*

ELLA: *You made your bed and now you have to deprive yourself of my company.*

ELLA: *Speaking of which, my parents are coming down to Manhattan for the weekend. My dad has some back-room political meetings he has to attend and so I'll be spending the weekend with them.*

JOSH: *They just had you for four whole days.*

ELLA: *They are the parental units.*

JOSH: *Do I finally get to meet the Carlsons?*

6

ELLA: Not on your life. I don't want to mention that you and I are seeing each other so if you want me, you'll have to come by late at night after my daughterly duties are finished.

JOSH: I'm insulted. Why don't you want me to meet your parents?

ELLA: My father is a notorious fourth-degree kind of man.

JOSH: Oh, yeah? You don't trust me to stand up to his scrutiny? I'm crushed...

ELLA: I don't want any drama. Besides, my mother will pester me to no end about you. I don't need the aggravation.

JOSH: I feel somehow slighted. But as long as I get you at night, I guess I'll take what I can get.

ELLA: I'll be yours from, say, nine-thirty at night until breakfast. I'll probably meet them for breakfast before my father's meetings and then will be with my mother the rest of the time until after dinner.

JOSH: I'll find something else to do with myself until nine-thirty. But I am disappointed. I would have liked to meet your parents. Your father is notorious.

ELLA: That's exactly why I'd rather not spring you on them at the moment. He is notorious.

JOSH: Okay. If that's what you want. Just so you know, I clean up pretty decently when I have to meet important people. I know what fork to use and all that...

ELLA: Josh! It's not that I don't think you'd pass muster, but I just don't want this weekend to be all about my new boyfriend.

JOSH: So, I take it that I am your new boyfriend? I'm beyond the fuck-toy stage and I'm now into the regular squeeze category?

ELLA: Regular squeeze sounds about right, although I do like the fuck-toy stage, too.

JOSH: It was a lot of fun, I have to admit.

ELLA: It was. Now, I have to go so quit distracting me or my boss will have my hide.

JOSH: That damn boss... Can I stop by later? I'll be on that floor for something.

ELLA: Okay but you should have an excuse. I don't want the whole office to know we're seeing each other.

JOSH: That's twice I've been crushed in this one textual exchange, Ella. I'm feeling a little insulted here...

ELLA: People know about my past. They know about your past. They'll think we're both crazy for seeing each other.

JOSH: Okay...I'm stopping by and will be in and out in two minutes tops. A quick kiss and grope are all I need.

ELLA: That I can give. Anytime. Now, I have to go and get work done. I hear the big boss is a real stickler for productivity.

JOSH: I've only heard nice things about him.

ELLA: Later. :)

I PUT MY CELL AWAY, SMILING AT OUR EXCHANGE. HE WAS always in a good mood, and was always a bit playful, which I enjoyed. He made me happy.

For the rest of the day, I waited for him to pop by and by the end of the day when he still hadn't, I felt a bit glum. While I didn't want the entire office staff to know I was seeing the big boss, I didn't mind him popping by for a quick kiss and squeeze. He could always find some reason to pop in to see Sharon or something. They were friendly enough that he could always use that excuse.

At five thirty, which was the official end of my day, I gathered up my things and said goodnight to Amber, who was working the front desk. I took the elevator down to the main floor and made my way out of the building. As I left the front door, I was accosted by Josh, who stepped out from behind one of the columns at the front of the building. He laughed when I squealed and pulled me into his arms.

We kissed, our focus completely on each other, while people walked around us on the sidewalk.

"I didn't think you were going to show up," I said when the kiss ended.

"I wanted to keep you in suspense."

"You wanted to tease me," I said, and gave him side-eyes. "You were making me all excited, wondering when you'd show up and what you'd do."

"I admit it. Anticipation makes it always so much more exciting. Now, how about some dinner? Since I'm going to be deprived of you as a dinner companion all weekend, I'd like to get in as much time as possible for the next couple of days."

"I'm all yours," I replied and stepped onto my tip-toes to kiss him.

"I like that." He kissed me back.

When we were finished, he took my hand and together, we walked along the street to his car, which was parked about a block away from the building.

He opened the passenger door for me and I got inside. After he got in beside me, he took my hand and kissed my knuckles.

"What do you feel like? Something healthy or some junk?"

"Mmm," I said and tried to think of what I wanted to eat. "Something junky. My mother is a health nut and so we'll probably be eating clean all weekend."

"How about some of Uncle Joe's Barbecue?"

"Perfect."

We drove off and went to Uncle Joe's, which was one of Josh's favorite restaurants. It was a tiny hole in the wall that looked like it belonged down by the bayou in Louisiana instead of Manhattan. He'd taken me there twice before and the food was so good, and there was always too much of it. I took home leftovers and ate them on my lunch break the next day, so it was a way for a single girl to stock my fridge for a meal or two.

We arrived at the restaurant and went inside, taking a tiny table beside the window looking out over Lexington. It was busy outside, and we were lucky to get in without a wait, but we'd chosen the best time to go. Most people got off work at six, so we beat the usual rush which really got started around six thirty or seven o'clock.

Josh ordered for us, and we sat and held hands across the table, watching outside and talking about the day while we waited for our food to come.

"I'm curious," Josh said, his tone becoming a little hesitant. "Why you're trying to avoid me meeting your parents. Is it too soon? We've been dating since September. I know your father was heavily invested in Jerkface as his future son in law, but still, I'd think he'd be happy to see you meet someone new. I clean up pretty well, all things considered..."

I sighed, not wanting to get into the whole business about his father's television reporters doing a big expose on one of my father's business partners.

"It's too soon," I said and squeezed his hand. "Let's just enjoy ourselves."

"I'd like to meet the Governor of New Hampshire one of these days," he said. "So, I hope that the next time they come to town, you bring me along. What about Christmas? That would be a good time to meet the parents."

"We'll see." I smiled and nodded, not committing to anything. He seemed assured that we'd still be together at Christmas, which was still three weeks away. That was a long time in a new relationship and after the nightmare that was my previous romance, I wanted to be cautious without too many expectations. Not that I was already thinking of us breaking up, but the chances of us being long-term partners was pretty slim. Even I had to admit that.

I didn't want to tempt the Gods, so I smiled and diverted the conversation to *The Chronicle* and how the search for good staff was going. Luckily, Josh was only too happy to tell me about his work staffing the new paper.

For the rest of the evening, I tried to just enjoy Josh in the moment instead of thinking ahead to what might or might not happen between us. I didn't want to hope too much.

I'd made that mistake before and wasn't going to make it again.

2

JOSH

"Stay at my place tonight," I said when we got back into the car after our meal. "I'd come to yours, but my neck gets cricked when we sleep on your bed."

"We've spent almost every night since we met at your place," Ella said with a coy smile. "I'm paying good money for my place in Chelsea. If I stay at your place every night, I'm throwing my money away."

"You could always move in with me." I kissed her knuckles. That didn't seem to please her as much as it did me.

She shook her head. "I love my place," she said softly.

"I understand." I knew that it was too soon to invite her to live with me, but it just slipped out. "Just stay with me at my place tonight. We can stop by your place and pick up a change of clothes if that's what worries you."

She nodded and glanced away. I kicked myself for making the offer but for some reason, the words just flowed so easily off my brain and into my mouth.

Move in with me.

13

I didn't know why but living with Ella felt natural to me. Like we fit together perfectly.

We drove to her place and she got out and went upstairs while I waited in the car. I didn't want to move too fast with Ella, despite feeling completely certain that I wanted her in my life.

In my bed. Every night.

She was still hesitant, and I understood why. Both of us had been burned by our previous relationships. While I was ready to jump right back in and give it another good try, she was still burned by her experience.

I had to be patient.

Luckily, patience was one of my virtues. I could wait her out. I'd just have to give her the room and time to figure it out for herself.

As I was sitting there, I noticed a man in a doorway in the building next to Ella's. He wore a dark raincoat and a black fedora with a feather in the brim. The hat and that feather made me think about my father, and a wave of nostalgia passed through me.

I wished he were still alive and was here to talk to me when I needed advice about the business or on personal issues. I would have loved if he could meet Ella and know that things were good for me on that front again. I knew he would have liked Ella and found her lovely and charming as I did.

Ella came out with a small overnight bag and jumped back into the car, smiling at me. I took her hand and we drove off back towards Mid-Town, the man in the black fedora forgotten. We parked in the parking garage and walked hand-in-hand to the entrance. The sky was dark, the air was cool, and the crowds on the street had thinned quite a bit.

"Would my lady like a nice horse and carriage ride around Central Park one of these fine nights?" I asked, when I saw one of the carriages drive by.

"That would be fun," she said. "But I hope it's not like the trip that took place on Seinfeld..."

I laughed at that, remembering the episode in question. "I'll make sure that the horse is fed oats and not Beef-O-Reeno."

"It's a deal," she replied.

WE WENT UP TO MY APARTMENT AND REMOVED OUR coats and shoes.

"Would you like a glass of wine or something to drink?" I went to the kitchen and opened the refrigerator.

"I'm good," she said and yawned, stretching her arms over her head. "I have an early day tomorrow. Better not have anything to drink."

I went back to her and pulled her into my arms.

"So do I." I bent down to kiss her, pressing my body against hers. Just the feel of her soft curves against me made me instantly hard, and I kissed her deeply, impatient to have her in my bed, naked. She responded, her arms tightening around my neck, her kiss just as passionate.

I carried her to my bedroom and we undressed each other, both of us eager to see each other naked, and to enjoy each other as quickly as we could.

The first time was fast for us both and was a blur of mouths and tongues and passion. We lay in each other's arms afterwards, her head on my shoulder, her fingers playing with the hairs on my chest.

"That was so good," she said with a sigh. "I feel spoiled."

"You deserve to be spoiled." I stroked her shoulder, enjoying the softness of her skin.

She rolled over on top of me and stared down into my eyes. "You're very good," she said softly, kissing me. "You're better than very good."

"You're just a hot little thing that I can't help but be good as a result."

"I can't help but want to devour every inch of you," she said, kissing my chin and jaw. "And there are lots of inches to devour."

I smiled and brushed back her hair from her face. "I'm all yours to devour any time you feel like it."

In fact, just her saying that had me ready again.

She began kissing me all over, moving down from my jaw to my shoulders and chest, over my abs and then lower still. I was hard as rock when she reached my cock and licked me from the base to the head, which she took into her mouth.

That was my last coherent thought for the next half hour.

WE SLEPT LIKE LOGS AND WERE STARTLED AWAKE BY THE clock radio alarm on the bedside table. I rolled over and shut it off and before I could grab her and kiss her good morning, she snuck out from under the covers and ran to the bathroom. I'd grown used to her attempts to avoid me in the morning, rushing to the bathroom to quickly brush her teeth and have a pee.

I smiled to myself and followed her inside, standing naked beside her, smiling as I caught her eye in the mirror. I grabbed my toothbrush and followed suit, brushing my teeth as well. We had enough time before work for another round,

16

if she was interested. I'd learn soon enough one way or the other.

I turned on the shower and stepped in and then when the water was right, I invited her in.

"Care to join me?" I asked, sighing as the hot water ran over my shoulders and down my body.

She crossed her arms and smiled. "If I do, will I actually get to shower, or did you have something else in mind?"

"Me?" I asked with mock-affront. "Are you impugning my motives, Ms. Carlson?"

I grabbed the bar of soap and began to lather my chest, the soap suds sliding down my body. Her eyes traveled over me, lingering over my now-thickening erection. She glanced up and smiled when she caught my eyes.

"I know exactly what your motives are, Mr. Macintyre. They are clearly corrupt."

"Can you at least help a man out and wash my... back?" I said with a grin. I turned my back towards her and waited. She'd complimented me previously on my glutes, so I flexed them.

"You are such a tease," she said and stepped into the shower. She pressed her body against me, her arms slipping around my waist, running up and down my chest and abs. "Let me have that bar of soap."

She took over and began washing me and soon, getting clean was the last thing on our minds.

SHE KISSED ME BEFORE SHE LEFT THE APARTMENT. ON MY part, I was dressed and ready for my morning ride around the park, my riding suit on.

"I can't believe you still ride even when there's snow on the ground."

"It's an addiction," I admitted. "I need my daily high from the endorphins to face the day."

"I thought you had enough post-coital endorphins to face the day."

"Them, too," I said with a laugh. "You have time for breakfast so go ahead and stay as long as you want," I said, grabbing her for another kiss before she closed the door.

"I'm going to the coffee shop across the street. I like their bagels."

"I have bagels," I said, pouting.

"You're going for your ride and besides, I like their coffee. It's one of the perks of my day."

"Okay," I said with reluctance. "When will I see you again?"

"My parents come into town tonight," she said. "I'll probably be out until later. Maybe nine thirty or ten. I'll text you."

"I'm going away on Monday to LA," I said, wanting to spend as much time with her before I went away for a whole week.

"I know," she said and stopped. "We'll spend as much time together as we can before you go."

She kissed me once more and then she was gone.

The apartment felt so much emptier without her presence, but I had to smile to myself. We'd had another great night together.

I finished tying my running shoes and then grabbed my helmet and bike and went for my daily ride around the park.

. . .

MY DAY WAS FILLED WITH WORK, AND IT WAS GOOD because it kept my mind off Ella and whether I'd be seeing her that night. We'd been almost inseparable since the trip to Bali, and it was fine with me. She eased into my life and heart and I felt a sense of contentment that I hadn't felt in a long time. She was different from other women I'd been with since Christie and I split. The other women were like placeholders while I found another woman I could love. I felt it when I was with them.

Ella felt completely different. She was a woman with substance to her. I remembered Marcella's attempts to find partners for me and how none of them could compete with Ella in terms of my attraction to her and my desire to be with her. The chemistry was off the charts, but it was more than that. We shared a love of the written word, an interest in good writing, whether it was the latest book in our catalogue or the editorial page of *The Chronicle*.

I was tempted during the day to sneak down into Ella's office and surprise her, but I was honestly so busy that each time I thought about it, another call would shatter my plan, or my assistant would bring in another document for me to review. I almost cancelled a call so I could zip down and see Ella, but at the last minute, decided to stick to my guns and not bother her during the day.

She didn't want there to be any gossip about us in the office and I understood that wish completely. People would view her differently, suspecting that she was sucking up to the big boss. Any advancement she made would be seen as due to the relationship. Besides, it just wasn't pleasant to have people talking about you behind your back.

I knew all about that.

I'd spent the last year trying to get over it myself. There had been a great deal of gossip in the office after Christine and I split, with various camps forming -- those who were on her side and those on mine. It wasn't something I'd wish on anyone.

BY THE TIME I WAS READY TO LEAVE THE OFFICE FOR THE night, it was after seven, and I hadn't heard from Ella all day. I was planning on grabbing some takeout and watching the game while I waited for a text from her about whether she was going to come by to spend the night with me when I got a text from Keith.

KEITH: Hey, old man. I haven't had a beer with you for ages. Come down to O'Malley's after work and have a pint.

I smiled to myself. Keith was right -- since Ella and I started seeing each other, I'd missed quite a few drinks with the boys.

JOSH: I'll see you in half an hour.

KEITH: Great! I actually didn't expect you to say yes, but I thought I'd give it a try. We'll be pleased to have you join us.

JOSH: Who's we?

KEITH: Just some people from the office. See you soon.

I put my cell away and went up to my apartment, changing into a more causal pair of jeans, black turtleneck and a black sports jacket. I checked my messages once before I left, but there was still nothing from Ella. I was almost going to send her a text but changed my mind at the last minute.

Nope. She was busy all evening. If we ended up together, it would be great. If not, I'd enjoy myself with staff from the office and watch the game on the TV at O'Malley's.

Before I went, I got a text from a name I didn't recognize. The name read *Kara*, and a shock of adrenaline went through me. The only Kara I knew was the wife of a man I'd been in the service with years earlier.

Grant McNeil, a fellow intelligence officer in the Army while I was over in Afghanistan. We'd been great friends during my time in the service, and I had a fling with his little sister, unbeknownst to him.

His wife's name was Kara. They married after he returned from Afghanistan, and I remembered ribbing him about all that married sex he was going to enjoy.

I read the text with trepidation.

KARA: Hi, Joshua, we haven't met but Grant passed away three days ago, and I wanted to let people in his contacts know. The memorial will be held tomorrow in Alabama where he grew up. His parents live in Millbrook, which is just outside Montgomery, and the graveside memorial will be at the local cemetery.

I felt sick as I checked my calendar. I had planned on going to California on Monday, but I could probably change my schedule to go to Montgomery and get a rental car, drive to Millbrook, stop by the memorial to pay my respects. Then, I could fly to LA a little earlier than I initially planned.

I remembered there was a convention that weekend in LA on print journalism. I could catch the tail end of it on Sunday so it might work out quite well, all things considered.

I checked the airline and changed my tickets. Since Ella's parents were in town for the weekend, I figured she'd be busy enough with them.

A deep sense of gloom filled me at news of Grant's death. He was so young that I feared the worst. I googled his name and came up with an obituary that only said he had died suddenly and unexpectedly.

That could only mean one thing -- he was one more casualty of war.

I needed a drink.

O'MALLEY'S WAS ONE OF THOSE CLASSIC IRISH PUBS IN downtown Manhattan. The building was narrow, with exposed brick, industrial lighting and a magnificent bar imported from Ireland and set up to mimic the original back home in Dublin. The place was filled with patrons when I arrived, and the music was some version of Irish ballads.

On one side of the bar was a set of dart boards, and on the other were a dozen tables filled with patrons. The bar held a number of stools at which the regulars sat and drank. Keith was at a table near the dartboards, and I saw several other staff from work sitting with him.

Callie from the admin side of things was currently playing darts with Joe, one of the advertising managers. People were laughing and having a good time. They'd all been there for at least an hour before I arrived.

"There you are," Keith said when he saw me. "Come and have a seat." He pulled out one of the chairs and I sat down, glancing around the table, trying to put names to all the faces.

"You know everyone here except Jana," Keith said, naming everyone for me. He stopped at a new woman I'd never seen before and didn't remember hiring. "Jana is a friend from Columbia. We worked on *The Review* together."

"Ahh," I said and nodded in her direction. "Good to meet you."

The Review was Columbia's journalism student paper. Keith had worked on it before being hired by MBC. I suspected that this was Keith's way of having her audition for a job at *The Chronicle*. If Keith wanted her, I trusted his judgement.

"I've been wanting to introduce you to Jana," Keith said. "She was the editor of *The Review* the year after I left."

"Good to know," I said, ordering a scotch when the waitress came by.

Then, for the next fifteen minutes, she told us all about her year working as an intern for a small paper in Massachusetts, where she did her undergrad. While I was initially interested in her experiences, I started to zone out after it appeared she was going to keep telling us the day in and day out mundanities of her life in Washington while she covered some political controversy.

It wasn't that I didn't care about politics. It was that these smaller elections weren't really all that important to my view for *The Chronicle*. Plus, she seemed to really be pushing her credentials, talking about her connections to people at *The Post*.

"So, are you hoping to work for *The Post* when you graduate?"

"Not necessarily," she said and smiled. "I'll be graduating in the spring but I'm already looking. Keith said you're rebuilding *The Chronicle* from the ground up. That sounds exciting."

I nodded and smiled, although I wasn't sure I felt all that great about her. While I appreciated confidence in people, I also liked to meet people as humans first, and as job applicants when the time was appropriate. She didn't seem to realize that this wasn't a job interview. In other words, she was a bit too forceful too soon for my management style, which was pretty laid-back.

Okay, she was pushy.

I didn't like that in men or women. Ambition was good, but I wanted to be Josh first when I went to a bar for drinks. Not Joshua Macintyre, Jr., CEO of MBC and potential boss.

It was probably Keith's fault. He should have known me well enough to advise her not to hit on me for a job when I first sat down. Maybe she should try to be a human being first and then, later, ask me about whether I had any openings.

Keith knew I was recruiting for *The Chronicle*. Jana's lack of tact in a personal situation was a big turn-off for me. Even if she had the best credentials, I'd have to see her perform better in a business setting to ensure she would be of value to the paper before I'd hire her.

So, I put her in the maybe column -- if she showed that she could treat me like a human being. I didn't want to deny someone a position if they were highly qualified and as the editor of the student paper at Columbia, she had skills.

For the next hour, we talked about various things, played darts and watched the game on the big screen TV against the wall. Jana and I played a game of darts, and she was good, a skilled player. While we played, she continued to push herself as a great candidate for *The Chronicle*.

"You should contact my headhunter and get yourself on her list," I said and told her about Marcella, who was doing all the hiring for my paper.

"Why do we need a headhunter?" she asked, standing beside me with her hands on her hips. "I'm here right now. Let me come in for a job interview. I'll send you my resume. I'd be a great addition to the paper."

I laughed, amused by her obvious confidence. "She does all my screening. Give her a call. Submit your resume. She might be able to find you a job anywhere you're interested."

She stepped closer and leaned over to me.

"I'm interested in you." She actually raised her eyebrows suggestively.

"Me?" I said in surprise. "I thought you were looking for a job."

"Until then, I'm single," she said and sipped her drink.

I said nothing in reply. Obviously ambitious, she was also obviously hitting me up for more than just a job. Did she think she had to sleep with me to get a job?

That pretty much tanked her application.

I sat down when the game was over and took out my cell, checking to see if Ella had texted me.

She hadn't. So, I texted her.

JOSH: Help! I need to be rescued from extreme boredom...

In a few moments, Ella replied.

ELLA: Is the game that bad?

JOSH: No, I'm at O'Malley's with the crew and some people just want to talk shop. I want to see you. Come to my place tonight after you're done with the parental units. It's Friday and we can sleep in tomorrow on my nice big four poster bed...

ELLA: I'll see you at ten.

JOSH: SCORE!

ELLA: Haha! Yes, you will. See you at ten.

JOSH: See you.

I smiled to myself and put my cell away. Seeing Ella would help wash away the sadness at the news I'd heard earlier about Grant. I had thought that a couple of drinks with Keith and the gang would make me feel more mellow, but if anything, it only made me sadder. It all seemed so superficial.

It was nine and everyone was starting to get a little drunk. I turned down another drink when the waitress came by.

"Well, I gotta go," I said and stood up.

People turned to me, surprised that I was leaving when the party was only now really starting.

"Leaving so soon?" Jana asked, clearly unhappy about it.

"Got an early morning bike ride to take. See you folks in ten days. I'll be in California for a week."

We all said our goodbyes and I left the bar, happy to be on my way home to meet Ella.

Before I could get to my car, Jana caught up with me and stood really close.

"Hey, do you want some company?"

She leaned against me, her body pressed against my arm. I could smell the alcohol on her breath as she leaned even closer.

"Sorry," I said and opened the car door. "I already have someone waiting for me at home."

She pouted and stepped back. "Keith said you were single."

"Keith doesn't know everything about my private life."

"Oh, okay," she said and shrugged. "If you change your mind, I'm happy to fill any empty spots."

"I'll let you know."

Then I drove off, glad to be out of there.

3
ELLA

I met my parents at the hotel bar where my father was already on his first glass of scotch. My mother had her usual glass of wine and on my part, I had a soda and lime because I didn't want to drink anything until dinner. My father usually didn't drink in public, but in Manhattan, he'd be largely anonymous, so he could drink without concern about what people would think.

It was silly, but he tried to keep a very clean public persona.

"So, dear, tell us more about your new job," he asked, turning to me, his eyes inquisitive. "With all the relatives at the house over the weekend, we really didn't get much time to talk. How is it going?"

"Great," I said and told them about my first few months on the job and how I had read more manuscripts that I ever imagined. More manuscripts that would never see the light of day because there were just too many for us to publish. We had to find reasons to say no.

27

"So, you're working for the enemy," my father said when we moved to the dining room and took our seats at a nice table.

"He's dead, father," I said, for I knew exactly what he meant. He meant Josh's father, Joshua Macintyre, Sr. The founder of MBC, which was the parent company of Macintyre Broadcasting's publishing subsidiary, Dominion Publishing. "He's no longer the CEO. I'm not working for the enemy."

"His son took over, and from what I read, the apple didn't fall far from the tree."

I sighed, not wanting to get into a fight with my father about Josh.

"I'm sure his son wasn't involved in whatever it was that made you hate Macintyre, Sr. That was twenty years ago when he would be a kid."

"He bought *The Chronicle*, and my sources tell me he's going to turn it into another *Washington Post* if he can. Lots of political coverage. Hard-hitting political coverage. It's no secret that he's a Democrat. I expect he'll keep on his father's tradition of running down the state's conservative candidates like his father did."

"From what I've heard, he's a very principled guy and is a political moderate, not a member of either party. Just wants to run a decent paper. Restore *The Chronicle* to its former glory."

"Have you met him, dear?" my mother asked. "I heard he's single. Is he as good looking as his photo in the paper makes him look?"

I smiled at her and shook my head. Trust her to wonder whether I'd met him. I couldn't tell either of them that I was sleeping with him every night and had been for the past month.

"I've seen him around, but he's not involved in Dominion

Publishing. He hired someone to take over as CEO in his place. He's too busy with the other work."

"That's good," my father said.

"That's too bad," my mother said. At the same time.

We all laughed. It cut the tension and for the rest of the evening, our talk turned to other matters instead of Josh Macintyre, Jr. I felt very uncomfortable lying to them about him, but I knew I'd get the third degree if I admitted that I was seeing him.

My mother would be happy, of course, being the perpetual romantic that she was, but my father would hate it. I'd never hear the end of it and then I knew he'd insist on meeting Josh and would probably grill him about his father's television news coverage of the whole political scandal that put my father's former business partner in jail.

So, the lie was meant to keep the peace. If anything more developed with Josh, if we decided to move in together, I'd have to come clean, but until then, they didn't have to know I was not only friends with him, I was sleeping with him on a regular basis and would very soon be fucking his brains out.

Our dinner was enjoyable once we got off the topic of the Macintyre family, and I caught up with news from back home, who was doing what outlandish thing in New Hampshire politics, which I was familiar with because of my father and Jerkface. Who among my old friends was now engaged, or had a baby, or was getting a divorce. Who had a new job and who was going to Harvard or Yale.

"I've only been gone for three months," I said. "How can so much happen?"

Finally, at nine thirty, after we had coffee and dessert and ran out of steam and conversation, I said good night to them both and took a taxi to the building to meet Josh.

Yes, I felt incredibly guilty going to him after denying that I knew him and hiding from them that I was more than just an employee -- even if unpaid. Keeping the peace was more important at that point in my life than being honest. It went against my basic nature to tell a lie, but keeping the peace was also an important value.

I struggled with it. But only for a while. As soon as I got into the elevator and pressed the button for the penthouse, I pushed my parents out of my mind and imagined Josh waiting for me.

I had a key to Josh's apartment that he gave me the second week we were seriously dating so I could use it whenever I needed to. I had to admit we met during lunch a few times for a quick and passionate session of sex. I never expected I'd be like that with someone new so quickly, but there was something about Josh I couldn't deny.

He was a heady mix of passion and intensity that made sex even better. Plus, he was so fun. He loved to laugh and enjoyed when we would tease each other. For the first weeks, I walked around in a state of near constant lust whenever I would think of him and imagine the prospect of us spending the night together.

I arrived at his apartment at about quarter to ten and he was already there when I entered.

"You're here," I said when I entered the apartment. He was in the kitchen reading a paper on the kitchen island, a glass of something in his hand. He smiled and came to meet me at the entrance while I removed my shoes and jacket.

"I escaped as quickly as I could."

"Party was a flop?" I asked, slipping my arms around his neck. He had freshly showered and was dressed only in a white terry cloth robe. We kissed, and he smelled so good. Fresh and clean. Already, my body was beginning to ache for him.

"It was fine, but I had better things to do than play darts and talk to people about the Knicks."

"Aren't you going to ask me how my evening went?" I said, only half-serious as he pulled me down the hallway to the bedroom.

"Not on your life."

He pushed me back onto the bed and we laughed as we tumbled onto it and he tried to undress me. For the next hour, at least, I forgot all about my parents and the lie I was living. Finally naked, we kissed and that was the last I heard about the bar until later.

Much later.

AFTER, AS WE LAY BENEATH THE SHEETS, OUR ARMS AND legs entwined, we talked about my parents and the whole sordid business.

"Did you tell them about me?" Josh asked, his voice curious.

"No," I said and bit my bottom lip guiltily. I felt immediately bad that I hadn't by the way his face changed when he heard my answer.

"Afraid of big daddy, are you?" he said, his voice light, but I could sense an edge of disappointment in his tone.

"Yes," I replied. I traced the blue tribal tattoo on his bicep, wishing I could change the subject.

"Come on, Ella," he said, chiding me. "You're an adult. Your father holds no sway over you. You're living in Manhattan all on your own--"

"I had all my ID, cell and laptop stolen in my first week here."

"And you managed to get them all replaced without calling daddy. Plus, you have a job--"

"Unpaid internship," I corrected.

"You have a man crazy about you, waiting at your beck and call," he said and smiled, nuzzling his nose into my neck. He rolled over on top of me and settled comfortably between my thighs.

"I do," I said and kissed him.

"So, you should be able to be open about us to them. I'm not a crook or charlatan. I'm actually a bona fide businessman, with a degree in commerce and I'm a veteran. I'm gainfully employed, have some stock options, and will be starting my own charitable foundation soon. What's not to love?"

He grinned at me, his eyes twinkling. His hair, which was long on the top, fell into his eyes in this incredibly sexy way. I brushed it aside.

"Nothing, except your father's past with my father's business partner that got him sent to jail."

He made a sound in the back of his throat. "It was one of those Ivy League jails, where they have designer overalls and they work in their own gardens to grow organic food and have their own cells with television and Wi-Fi. Hardly much of a hardship. Besides, he broke the law."

"In my father's mind, his partner was set up and betrayed and your father orchestrated it."

"My father cooperated with the FBI. Your father's business

partner was guilty of insider trading," Josh said firmly. "That's illegal. He was found out in part because of reporters at my father's news corporation. Your father should be happy that the rule of law prevailed."

"I agree, but he felt that his partner was set up, and was entrapped by a traitor. He hadn't been involved in any kind of criminal act prior to the deal in question."

"If you were offered the chance to make a million dollars by breaking the law, would you do it?"

"No," I said and frowned. "Of course not."

"Well, your father's business partner did. He had the chance to say no, but he didn't." Josh raised his eyebrows and waited for my reply.

Of course, he was right. I always thought that my father's partner deserved what he got because he did cheat. He broke the law and made millions because he had insider knowledge and used it to sell stocks and make a fortune, but my father was loyal to a fault. That meant he never forgave the news organization and the CEO, who directly approved the sting.

Joshua Macintyre, Sr., in other words.

If Josh and I were going to continue to see each other, and I truly hoped we would, I would have to fess up eventually. It was just one of those uncomfortable family conversations I did not want to have.

I would one day, if it came to that, but at that moment, Josh and I were still too new to each other to rock the family boat.

"I'll tell my parents one of these days, when the time is right. Not until."

"Okay," Josh said, and I could hear the resignation in his voice. "You can decide how to deal with your parents. I wish I still had some."

He gave me a look, which said his father's recent passing still hurt.

I kissed him, sympathy for him filling me. As much as my father and I locked horns on occasion, and my mother exasperated me, I loved them both. I couldn't imagine being so young and having no father or mother. It explained why he was so close to his brothers.

JOSH WOKE UP IN THE NIGHT IN A SWEAT. IT WASN'T THE first time, but it still shocked me.

"What?" I asked, my arm around his shoulder.

He shook his head and ran a hand through his hair. "Just a bad dream."

"That's another one. Three this past two weeks. Are you under a lot of stress or something?"

He shrugged. "I got some bad news. A fellow intelligence officer who was in Afghanistan with me died. I'm actually going to his memorial today and will fly right to LA to spend time with David. That probably gave me the nightmare."

"What happened to him?" I asked, lying back down beside Josh when he did. "He's pretty young to die."

"I think he killed himself," Josh said, his voice soft. "The obit read suddenly and unexpectedly. That's usually a sign of an accidental death or suicide."

"I'm so sorry," I said and kissed him.

It took a while for us both to fall back asleep.

THE NEXT MORNING, VERY EARLY BECAUSE JOSH HAD AN 8:00 a.m., flight, we had a quick shower and a love-making session that had both our hearts pumping from exertion. Then, we sat at the kitchen island and had breakfast. Josh scrambled some eggs and made toast, while I made the coffee.

Despite the early hour, it was an entirely comfortable domestic scene and I smiled to myself as I poured us each a cup.

"What are you smiling about?" Josh asked when he saw me. He came over after placing our plates on the counter and pulled me into his arms.

"I was just thinking that you'd make a good Tarzan."

"What?" he asked, grinning widely. "Are you saying I'm a wild man of the jungle? I just had my hair cut and my beard trimmed. I am anything but Tarzan."

"Those boxer briefs," I said and glanced down at them. They were leopard pattern and nicely fit his well-developed biker butt and thighs. "You're buff. And that tribal tattoo. All you need is a man bun."

"Never!" he said with a laugh, kissing me. "No man bun for me. I'd be laughed out of the boardroom."

I ran my fingers through his hair, which was much longer on top and buzzed shorter on the sides. "I can almost make one, if I had an elastic band..."

"Get thee behind me, Devil Woman!" he said and wrestled my hands away from his hair. "You won't get a man bun on me if I can help it."

"Aww, that's too bad," I said with a giggle, when he turned me around in his arms, pinning me in an embrace. "You'd look so incredibly sexy."

"You don't find me sexy now?" he murmured, his lips at my ear, his breath hot on my skin.

"You're incredibly sexy. In fact, you're a babe," I said. Then, I laughed out loud when he tickled me under my ribs.

"A babe?" he said, mock-indignant. "I'll have you know I've been told I'm handsome in a boyish way."

"Who told you that?" I asked, actually curious.

"A scout for a modeling agency tried to recruit me when I was seventeen and was at one of the fashion shows with my mom."

He let go of me and I turned around in his arms, clasping my hands around his neck. "You were? You're very handsome but not in a boyish way any longer. You're just plain handsome in a manly kind of way."

"Manly," he said with a smile and bent down to kiss me. "What am I going to do without you for a whole week? Are you sure you can't convince Sharon to let you take a vacation?"

I sighed and kissed him back. "No can do. We have this slave driver of a CEO who wants the Spring Lineup finished before the end of the month."

"What a bastard," he said and sighed, pressing his lips against my forehead. "Maybe they should replace him."

"I heard he has an arm's-length relationship with the book publishing business, but he still demands we meet all our deadlines."

We stood still in each other's arms and just enjoyed the moment. Josh was going away for a week to LA to do whatever it was he was doing there, which he had postponed for over a month after we started being a regular thing. He'd pushed it back and back and finally, told me he had to go this week, or he'd be behind schedule.

I didn't want to see him go, and would miss him, but it would give me a week to get caught up with my own writing, which I'd put on the back burner since we started seeing each other.

"What will I do without you?" he asked, brushing hair off my cheek. "I'll have to resort to the old manual method."

"It's a tried and tested method," I said with a grin. "You have Mr. Manuel. I have B.O.B."

"Oh, God. Maybe we can do phone sex."

"How about Skype sex? I'd like to watch you," I said, raising my eyebrows playfully.

"I'd like to watch you watching me watch you," he replied, grinning. He bent down and kissed me.

"It's a date. Call me just before you're ready for sleep and we can sext each other."

He pulled me tightly against his body and we hugged.

"Now, unfortunately, I have to finish packing and take a taxi to the airport."

"And I should go back to my place and get ready to meet my parents for lunch."

We kissed once more and went about our various tasks. I finished dressing and gathered up my things and went to him for one last kiss and hug before I left.

"Have a good trip," I said, smiling up at him while he pulled on his jacket. "I'm sorry it has to start out so sad for you."

"Me, too. Have a good week," he replied and kissed me deeply once more.

Then I left the penthouse and went down the elevator, a sense of sadness that I wouldn't be with him for a full week.

I kicked myself mentally. We'd talk every night and probably text each other. Plus, the sexting.

I'd manage fine...

4
JOSH

My early flight to Montgomery gave me some time to read more about Grant's death.

Apparently, he was involved in a single vehicle crash that killed him early on the previous Tuesday morning. That made me feel somewhat better, in a strange way. Maybe he didn't kill himself after all. The accident happened early in the morning so perhaps he had fallen asleep at the wheel and went into the ditch.

I rented an SUV and drove to the Millbrook cemetery just in time for the service. I found my way to the family row of seats and went to Mr. and Mrs. McNeil so I could pay my respects.

We exchanged a few words, and they thanked me for coming. I sat in a seat in the back and waited for the service to start, checking around for Grant's little sister, Penny, but she wasn't there. That surprised me. Grant and Penny were very close so I would expect her to show up.

Finally, just a couple of minutes before the service was

scheduled to start, Penny arrived, stumbling over from the road that circled the small cemetery. I felt bad when I saw she was either drunk or stoned. Her long blonde hair was still wet as if she had just come out of the shower moments before. Her dress was wrinkled, and her shoes were spike heels that sunk into the soft grass, making her gait even more unsteady.

"Sorry, everybody," she said, her voice audibly slurred, "but as usual I'm the one holding up everything."

She went over and sat beside her father and the pastor began the service.

He spoke of Grant's service to the country, and his heroism. How he'd struggled after he returned to find his place in society and how the community had failed him, noting that Grant waited for months to get an appointment for mental health care.

I knew then that the accident wasn't an accident after all. In the end, he had taken his life when he couldn't find the help he needed. It was a familiar story to those of us who came back from the war.

When the sermon was finished, we each threw a shovelfull of dirt over his coffin. Afterward, we went to the McNeil home on the outskirts of Millbrook. There, in the old rancher Mr. McNeil had built himself, we had coffee and a light lunch of sandwiches and small cakes. I spoke with Mr. and Mrs. McNeil, reminiscing about my time with Grant in Afghanistan.

While we were speaking, a commotion erupted in the other room, and I heard a woman's shrill voice, clearly distraught. I went to the kitchen and it was Penny. She was standing at the sink, facing a man I didn't recognize.

"He killed himself okay?" she said to the man, her eyes tearful. "He was a fucking hero. The army made him do bad things over there and he couldn't live with it. He *hated* the war. He *hated* it. It killed him."

"*Penelope*," her mother said in a hushed voice. "Get control over yourself. For God's sake..."

"Well, it did!" Penny said, her eyes wide, her face flushed.

I went over to her. "Hey," I said and put my hands on her shoulders. "Are you okay? Maybe we should get you out of here."

"Oh, it's *you*," she said when she recognized me. "Mr. Richie Rich himself. The one who got away. Sure, you can help me. You could have married me instead of leading me on."

I frowned, for while we had fucked a dozen or so times when I was in Montgomery on leave with Grant, she never gave me any sense that she thought it was anything more than fun.

I pulled her to the rear of the house, finding a long hallway and taking her to the back, away from the other guests. She was clearly drunk or high, and while I understood that people dealt with grief differently, I had a feeling this was something common for her.

"Let's get you somewhere quiet," I said and took her into the back room. I glanced around and realized it had been Grant's bedroom when he was a boy. On the walls were diplomas and ribbons from track and field meets and baseball games. On the shelf were trophies from when Grant was involved in high school sports. The walls were filled with pictures of him from his days in the military. On a shelf were pictures of him with his wife and two boys.

I felt a choke in my throat when I saw a photograph of him with his boys...

Penelope sat on the bed and cried, wiping her eyes and shaking her head. "I can't believe he's gone."

I sat beside her and took her hand in mine, wanting to comfort her. When I did, the sleeve of her dress pulled up and I saw track marks on the soft skin on the inside of her forearm.

She was an addict.

What had happened to her in the time between our last meeting and now?

It had been three years since I slept with her, but she looked so much older when I saw her up close. Her skin was sallow, and her teeth looked stained and one was chipped.

Mrs. McNeil came inside and saw us sitting side by side on the bed.

"Trust you to always make a mess of everything," Mrs. McNeil said, her hands on her hips. "Why did you have to talk about it like that? People don't want to know."

"They should know," Penelope said. "They need to know 'cause it's just going to keep happening."

Penelope turned to me and slipped her arms around me, weeping into my shoulder.

Mrs. McNeil shook her head. "She should leave. She's in no shape to be here. Can you take her home?"

I nodded. "Sure. No problem."

I stood and pulled Penelope up, leading her to the back door. Before I did, I stopped and extended my hand to Mrs. McNeil.

"I'm so sorry about Grant," I said.

"We all are," she replied and clasped my hand.

. . .

PENNY AND I LEFT THE HOUSE AND I GOT HER SEATED IN the SUV, entering her address on the other side of town in the car's navigation system. When we arrived at her place, I was shocked to see was a run-down heap that looked like an old rooming house.

"This is it?" I asked, horrified that she was living there.

"Yeah, some of us don't have billions of dollars," she said and stumbled up the front steps to the front door. I followed her up the stairs, wanting to see where she lived and if she was going to be safe.

Inside, we went up to the second floor and a rear bedroom that was where she lived. The house had been divided up into suites and she had a single room with a hot plate and mini fridge. There was a bed against one wall and a chair in front of a television.

I checked the refrigerator. There was nothing inside except some moldy leftover pizza and a few bottles of condiments. Drug paraphernalia littered the kitchen table, including syringes, spoons and a candle plus a lighter and some foil. An ashtray overflowing with cigarette butts topped it off.

"Are you going to be okay?" I asked, checking my watch. "I have a flight to catch to LA."

"Yeah, I'll be okay." She glanced away, not meeting my eyes. I turned to the door, feeling bad at leaving her but I had to get to the airport soon.

"That's what Grant always said, too," she muttered under her breath.

I turned back. "If you need help, I can call someone," I said when she sat down on her chair and held her head in her hands.

"The only thing I need is twenty bucks, so I can get high,"

43

she replied and looked up, meeting my eyes. Hers were red and she looked desperate.

I reached into my pocket and pulled out my wallet. I thumbed through my bills and took out one hundred in twenties.

"Here," I said. "Get some food. Take care of yourself. Get some help, Pen."

"Get some help," she said and took the money. I could practically see the wheels turning in her mind as she counted out the bills. She was likely figuring out how much of a party she could have on that money. "You think this will help me? All it will do is keep me from being sick for a few days."

I held my hands up, realizing what she said was true but not knowing what I could do in that moment to truly help her.

"Give me a call or email me if you need anything," I said. "I can wire you some money."

"Okay," she said, and she looked up at me. I saw some small bit of gratitude in her eyes, but there was also a deep sense of helplessness in them as well.

Like she was lost and she knew it.

I left the house, walked down the stairs to the SUV, a sick feeling in my stomach.

The drive to the airport in Montgomery took me back past the cemetery and I saw the mound of dirt where Grant's body was buried. Sadness filled me at the carnage left by the wars on people back home.

It was then I got the idea for the foundation I would start and run. It would be in Grant's memory and would provide for mental health care for returning veterans and their families. If I could stop one vet with PTSD from killing himself, maybe, *maybe*, all my father's money might be of some value.

· · ·

MY FLIGHT TO LAX WAS UNEVENTFUL, WHICH WAS JUST the way I liked it.

I had a first-class seat on an American Airlines flight, and spent my time writing a long email to my accountant at MBC, asking him about doing the work to set up a foundation in Grant's memory. I detailed what I wanted the foundation to do and asked him to do the leg work figuring out what needed to be done to get it up and running.

The rest of the flight I spent reading the latest newspaper, trying to get my head around the meetings I'd have all day at the new office. There was a convention in town and I was attending several sessions to meet with other news types and learn what was the latest thinking in keeping the print news business alive.

I'd take a taxi right to the convention center, where I'd have a room, and would spend the following morning attending the closing session. Sunday after lunch, I'd drive to David's mansion in the Hollywood Hills. We'd made this plan months earlier, and now, finally, I was there and the timing around the convention made me glad I'd put the trip off. It gave me the chance to attend Grant's memorial service and take care of Penelope.

There'd be a lot of hard partying at David's place once the EP was finished, but I wasn't up to it. Not after my experience in Millbrook.

David was in the middle of recording a new EP and so interspersed between recording sessions, we could catch up. I loved to listen to David and his band practice. He got all the musical talent in our family, taking after our mother. I got business sense from my father.

Luckily, that meant there was no competition between us

and we could just be brothers.

I ARRIVED AT THE CONVENTION CENTER JUST IN TIME FOR a Skype session with Ella.

I glanced at my watch, calculating how late it was back in Manhattan. It was then I saw a text from Ella.

ELLA: Hey, Tarzan, it's me, Jane. How's the Jungle?

I smiled.

JOSH: Getting ready to swing my way up to my room. Hang on.

It was midnight in Manhattan and I expected Ella would be really tired and wanting whatever sexting we were going to do to get started.

ELLA: I'm waiting with bated breath...

JOSH: Skype me. I'm more than ready.

I had never had Skype sex before and was curious how it would go. I opened my laptop and sure enough, in a couple of minutes, Ella Skyped me and a window opened on my laptop screen.

She was there in all her glory, lying back on her bed, holding her cell up so I could take her delicious nakedness in.

"God, you're a sight for sore eyes," I said appreciatively.

"Show me how excited you are to see me," she said in a breathy voice.

So I did, angling my cell down so she could see just how excited I was...

I saw her eyes widen in appreciation of my very erect and excited cock, which I had in my hand and was slowly stroking.

"Spread your legs and let me see you touch yourself," I said, my voice commanding.

She did, and my dick jumped in my hand when I saw her slip two fingers between her lips to stroke her clit. She was nice and wet and ready.

"Damn, I wish I was there, so I could lick you," I said with an appreciative groan.

"Oh, God, I wish you were here, so you could lick me, too," she said and flashed me her eyes, and then moved her cell lower so I could see her breasts, her erect nipples, and then her hand once more, her fingers stroking herself.

I stroked my cock a bit more intently while I imagined her using a dildo on herself.

"I want to see you use B.O.B.," I said, breathlessly.

"You do, do you?" she replied, her own voice breathless. "I happen to have it right here."

She pulled out a flesh-colored dildo, which was impressive and slightly wobbly in her hand. I watched, open mouthed, while she slid it against her clit.

"That's nice," I said, my hand moving over my dick, spreading some fluid over the head, wishing it was her mouth or it was inside of her silky hotness.

"You like this?" she asked and slowly pushed the head of the dildo inside of her.

I groaned. "Oh, yes, I do. Very much. Fuck yourself with it."

She fumbled with the cell, trying to find a place for it that would allow her to use both hands. Finally, after several failed attempts, she managed to perch it on the bed in such a way that I could see her groin while she slid the dildo inside and played with her clit.

"This won't take long," I managed, between gritted teeth.

"Me either," she replied.

Both of us pleasured ourselves while we watched each other and soon, she was tensing up the way she did when she was just about to come.

"I'm going to..." she said, her voice tense.

"Oh, God," I groaned. "Let me see you come. Let me see your face."

She turned to face the camera, adjusting it, and then I watched while she came, her body arcing in, her fingers slowing over her clit, the dildo remaining inside of her. I heard her gasping, breathing out as she orgasmed.

It sent me over and I pulled hard on my cock until the first waves of my orgasm began and I ejaculated, my eyes practically rolling back in my head. I wanted to watch her face while I came, so I struggled to keep my eyes open.

Finally finished, I leaned back in the chair, my throbbing dick still in my hand.

"God, that was better than I imagined," I said, smiling. I watched while she removed the dildo and lay on her side, facing the camera.

"It was good, wasn't it?" she managed, smiling back. "I've never done that before."

"Me, neither," I replied. "Not exactly like that."

Her eyes widened. "You have sexted before?"

"A couple of times," I said and grabbed a tissue, wiping myself off. "But not like this."

"I wish you were here, so we could snuggle," she said and pouted. "I've grown accustomed to your presence in my bed. Or should I say, in your bed."

"Me, too," I replied. "We'll do this every night if you want."

She smiled. "If I want..."

48

"Well, I definitely want it. Skype sex like this is a keeper."

She yawned. "I better go to sleep. Early morning with mom and dad."

"Okay," I said. "I'll be in sessions all day and there's a late session on Sunday night so I probably won't have much time to Skype with you, but you should text me or we can talk."

"I will."

"Good night, Ella. I miss you."

"Good night, Josh. I miss you too."

The session ended, and I sat there for another moment, recovering from my orgasm. It dulled the sense of gloom that had pervaded my mind since I'd learned about Grant's suicide but only just. I had another quick shower and went to bed, thinking to myself about Ella's and my session of mutual masturbation.

It wasn't the real thing, but it was the next best.

THE FOLLOWING DAY WENT FAST, WITH ME KEEPING BUSY attending sessions in the morning, afternoon and evening.

The dinner session was on print journalism in the twenty-first century digital age. Afterwards, I met a few colleagues in the business for drinks.

We spent the next hour talking news, and I loved every moment of it, eager to learn from others in the field and to share what we were doing with *The Chronicle*.

"You're ambitious to try to revive it," Callie Summers, a newspaper owner from Idaho said.

"Ambitious, but also maybe foolish," I replied with a laugh. "It's expensive to find good talent. It's the biggest expense, but the most important."

Callie was a bit older than me, attractive in a very calculated way. She'd sat beside me and tried to engage me in a side conversation several times. I answered her perfunctorily to be polite, but I was more interested in the larger conversation and would turn back as soon as I could.

We talked shop for a while longer, and when I saw it was already ten thirty, I'd had enough.

"Well, gentlemen and ladies," I said and stood, slipping my cell into my jacket pocket. "I must say goodnight. It's been a pleasure and if any of you are ever in Manhattan, please give me a call."

We said goodbye and I left the bar, walking to the elevators so I could go up to my room.

Callie followed me, rushing to catch up. When the doors opened, she got in beside me.

"You're leaving so soon," she said and stood close to me. "It's only nine. I hoped you and I could have a drink together, compare notes."

"I'm pretty tired," I replied, trying to be nice. "Maybe tomorrow between sessions."

"Care to come to my room and have a nightcap?" she asked, stepping even closer. She ran her fingers up my lapel and stroked my shoulder.

"Sorry," I said and removed her hand. "I'm seeing someone."

"So am I," she said in a very affected sultry voice. "What happens at conventions, stays at conventions is my motto."

I shook my head. "Sorry," I said and smiled. "I'm flattered that you're interested, but I value fidelity in all things, business and romance."

She pouted. "That's too bad," she said. "Your loss."

I didn't respond, not wanting to confirm or deny but then I

changed my mind. "Actually, My lover and I are going to Skype so don't worry about me. I'll be just fine."

"Ain't nothing like the real thing, baby," she said and shrugged. "If you change your mind and want something real and hot, I'm in room 912."

The elevator door opened and off she got. I smiled to myself as the doors closed, glad that our little encounter was over. She knew what she wanted and wasn't afraid to try for it. I guess business people had to be somewhat ambitious and unafraid of failure. If I hadn't been seeing Ella, I probably would have turned her down anyway. She was a bit too forward for my tastes. I preferred someone who I was mutually attracted to, and not just an easy fuck.

I got off the elevator at my floor and went to my room. I had a quick shower before sitting on my bed and checking my cell.

We had a nice chat and then, exhausted, I went to bed, missing her more than I thought possible.

ON MONDAY, I SLEPT IN LATE AND AFTER A QUICK shower, I checked my cell and saw that David had texted me.

DAVID: Hey, bro. I hope you're hungry tonight. I have a massive side of ribs that I'll put on the barbecue for dinner. I can't wait to see you, catch up.

JOSH: I can't wait to see you, too. The convention will be done for the day at four. Given traffic, I should be out there in time for dinner. See you soon.

When the final session was over and the moderator gave us a summary of the convention, I said goodbye to everyone I'd met and spent time with and left the convention room. I had checked out before noon and had my suitcase and briefcase with me. I got one of the clerks at the front desk to call me a limo and waited for it to arrive, so I could sit back and relax on the trip to Brentwood.

I ARRIVED AT CLOSE TO SIX O'CLOCK MONDAY AT DAVID'S mansion on a quiet treelined street. The villa was surrounded by tall junipers and palm trees. A security fence surrounded the villa and video cameras monitored the perimeter. The limo stopped at the gate and the driver spoke into the microphone, announcing my arrival.

The gate clicked open and swung back, admitting the vehicle to a circular driveway that led to the huge double front doors. The house itself was ostentatious, with huge columns like the place was a Greek temple. The villa itself was higher up on a hill and overlooked the city below. I was impressed.

The limo stopped at the front entry and the door opened. David came out, practically jumping on top of me when I got out of the rear passenger seat.

"There you are, big brother," he said and hugged me, kissing me on the cheek. "Come on in. Let me get your bag. You can finally see the new place."

He grabbed my suitcase when the limo driver opened the trunk while I grabbed my briefcase and together, we went inside the villa.

We entered its cool dim interior, which was several degrees cooler than the outside. Everything was marble and gilded antique. I hadn't been to his new place yet so was impressed with its lush interior. There was even a small waterfall in the huge entryway.

"A waterfall?" I said, standing in front of it.

"Water is calming," David said, standing beside me. "Listening to flowing water is supposed to reduce stress. Have you never heard of the blue mind hypothesis?"

"What?"

"It's a hypothesis that because our species survived beside the ocean, that being beside a large blue body of water makes us happy. Hearing the sound of the ocean or water on a shore reduces stress. The ocean is our mother, you know."

"Our mother? What kind of new-age BS is this?" I said in a half-joking way.

"It's definitely new-age BS but I like it. I don't believe the woo woo stuff, but I think water does make me happy. That's why I like to see the ocean and have a big pool outside and a waterfall in my entry. Come in and let's get you set up in your bedroom."

We went up the grand staircase that curved up to the second-floor landing. It was all very impressive, and it seemed a bit at odds with my younger brother's tastes in decorating, but he was growing up, despite the bad boy persona. The place was clean and quiet and altogether more grown up than his last place, which was much more the way I pictured a rock star to live. His old place had modern furniture, pool parties every weekend, a huge recording studio on the main floor where various musicians and hangers-on congregated at all hours. Skeevy looking promoters who were probably hoping to fleece the band of its hard-earned money.

This house was grown-up.

My room was bigger than Ella's whole studio apartment, with a massive king-sized four poster monster of a bed, brocade covers and dozens of pillows. A set of patio doors to a balcony overlooking the pool below. A huge en-suite bathroom with jet tub, two-person shower and separate john. There was a massive flatscreen TV across from the bed and even a small sofa and chair.

I wished, not for the last time, that Ella was with me, so we could enjoy the luxury together.

It wasn't that I was unfamiliar with luxury. I'd grown up with it, but it tickled me somehow to know that David had chosen this house and had it decorated to suit his tastes. My little brother...

I laid my suitcase on the bench at the end of the bed and turned to David.

"What's up for tonight?" I asked, leaning back against the bed frame.

"Not much," he said. "If you were hoping for a party, you'll have to wait for next weekend. We're practicing over the next couple of days before we lay down some new tracks."

"That's okay," I said and shook my head. "It's going to be a working visit for both of us. I'll be spending most of the day at the offices, trying to get caught up and meeting with my people. I'll be happy just to have meals with you and visit when you're free."

"Good," he said and came over. "What's up with that girl of yours?"

"What girl?" I asked with a grin. I'd already told David and my other brothers about Ella, but I enjoyed playing dumb.

"The one you fell for when I was there. The one who's making you smile right now. The one you wouldn't stop talking about over Thanksgiving dinner."

"She's fine. In fact, she's pretty amazing."

"Good, good. All the brothers are glad to see you getting back up on the saddle again, so to speak. Tell me about her. No, wait. Put your stuff away and come downstairs for a drink. We can talk by the pool. I have to do something first."

"Okay."

I spent a few moments hanging up my shirts and suits, and then went downstairs after changing into a pair of shorts and a t-shirt. It felt good to be in a warmer climate. I loved the sun and warmth of LA.

I went down to the main floor and David was already there, standing at the bar and placing two glasses on the counter.

"What'll you have?" he asked, waiting with his tongs ready to pick up ice. "You usually drink scotch on the rocks, if I'm not mistaken. Or craft beer."

"Beer would be nice," I said, and he pulled out a bottle of some local craft beer that I didn't recognize.

"This is good stuff," he said and cracked it open, handing me the open bottle. "You'll like it."

I took a sip and nodded in approval. I could feel the stress slipping away as David brought his own bottle of beer out and we went to the patio. Under a huge umbrella were two reclining chairs. We each took one and leaned back, sipping our beer and taking in the amazing scenery.

"This is the life," I said and sighed. "It's almost December and the weather is fantastic. Back in Manhattan, there's snow on the ground."

"That sucks. Move out here. You could spend winters here and go back to Manhattan in the spring."

I shook my head. "I could maybe come out for a couple of

weeks now and then, but I couldn't stay here for any length of time. The paper requires that I be there all week to oversee things. I want to be really involved. Not just a funder."

"I understand. Just me being greedy, wanting you guys to move out here. Now that dad's gone, we only have each other. Plus, our own families, of course. But you know what I mean. I don't want to lose touch with you guys."

"We won't," I said and gave his arm a squeeze. "We may not live in the same city, but we can all fly somewhere pretty fast if we want."

"So, tell me more about you and Ella. Did you take a picture at least, the way you promised?"

I laughed, because David was not going to let it go until I showed him a picture proving she was real and not just a story I told to convince them I was okay. I pulled out my cell and flipped through my pics of her, selecting one of her sitting on my desk at my apartment, wearing this soft white sweater and leggings, both of which amplified her curves. Her red-brown hair was long, and she was smiling at me. I smiled when I remembered taking it one afternoon when we'd just finished walking around Central Park and her cheeks were flushed. We made love very soon after the pic was taken.

"Here she is," I said and handed him the pic. "As promised."

"Wow," David said and looked closer. "She's lovely. I like the freckles. And dimples, too."

"She's sweet. And she's really smart and might go to Columbia next year to do her Masters. She's got a great sense of humor. And she writes erotica for fun and wants to be an author."

"You already told me all that," David said with a laugh, for

I had told him pretty much everything I knew about Ella. "She's kind of the exact opposite of Christie, isn't she?"

I frowned. "What do you mean?"

"You know, Christie was blonde and tall and model-slim. Business major. Wanted to be one of those Housewives of Manhattan or something and saw you as the way to get the lifestyle."

"Ella thought I was a bicycle courier."

David grinned. "See? Exact opposite of Christie. If Christie had thought you were only a bicycle courier, she would never have even spoken to you."

"That's the truth," I said.

"She saw you, found out who you were, and that was it, if I recall you meeting her."

"She was certainly ambitious." I rubbed my eyes, thinking of meeting Christie at a club three years earlier when I was just home from Afghanistan. She'd told me she asked around and found out who I was, then set me in her sights and came after me.

I'd been flattered that such an intelligent and obviously beautiful woman had come after me. She did everything she could to win me, even getting a job with me, slowly convincing me to start a relationship.

Of course, she didn't love me. She loved my lifestyle.

David handed me back my cell and I stared at the pic of Ella. So completely different from Christie. When I thought of Ella, I felt like she was real. She wasn't contrived in any way from her looks to her personality.

I wanted her to be with me pretty much every spare moment I had.

"You have to bring her out here, or I'll come there for a

weekend so I can meet her."

"We'll see," I said. But I smiled to myself. Yes, I had fallen for her. David had been right before, and he was right now.

"Aww," David said, unable to constrain himself. "You're a goner." David laughed, giving me a good-natured punch in the shoulder.

I laughed back, not afraid to admit it.

"I am."

I was.

5
ELLA

I met my parents for lunch at a famous deli down the street from the hotel. The place was busy with noon-hour patrons, and we were lucky to get in without a long wait.

We ordered the world-famous pastrami on rye sandwiches with matzo ball soup and had a nice hour talking about the city and my early experiences at Macintyre Publishing.

I filled them in on my duties and the Spring catalogue, and our plans for the following Fall lineup.

"What about your own writing?" my mother asked, always wanting me to write a romance novel. "Are you working on anything?"

I wouldn't confess to the erotica, of course, for it would shock my father to know his daughter wrote dirty stories, but I did tell them about my chick lit story, based loosely on my own broken heart. It was going to be a Bridget Jones style story of a woman who starts life over in the big city and finds that success and happiness is the best revenge.

At least, that's what I told them. I really hadn't had any

time to work on it since Josh and I started seeing each other. That was okay by me. I'd much rather have the real-life Mr. Big in bed with me than be writing about a fictional one.

AFTER OUR LUNCH WAS FINISHED, MY MOM WANTED TO go shopping while my dad had his party meetings. We did the usual trip along Fifth Avenue, and of course, I thought about how close the apartment was.

"Your office is around here isn't it?" she asked.

"It is. Just over there," I said and pointed to the old building.

We stopped at a Starbucks and had a coffee mid-afternoon.

"It's so exciting," she said, smiling as we sat in the window and watched the people walking by. "I know your father was upset that you left, but I was excited for you, even though I knew I'd miss you. To move to the Big Apple and live on your own. I could never have dreamed of doing it."

"It's great," I said, and it was then I decided to tell her the truth about my first rocky weeks in the city. "Actually, I had a few hard times when I first moved here."

I told her all about losing my backpack on my first day of work and how a bicycle courier had rescued me, helping me out with a cell phone and some spending money until I was able to get access to my bank.

"A bicycle courier?" she said, surprised. "Was he at least good looking?"

"Very," I said and wagged my eyebrows. "Steph called him a real babe."

"She did?" my mother said with a laugh. "Well, Steph would know. So, does this bicycle courier have a name?"

"Keith," I said, using the name of the guy who worked for Josh. I made up a story on the fly about him wanting to buy a company and be an entrepreneur one day.

"That's nice dear," my mother said, but I could tell by the sound of her voice that she didn't approve. "I'm sure you'll meet someone suitable when you go to Columbia."

I frowned. "Mom, women don't go to college to meet men."

"Of course, they don't," my mother said, her voice sounding tired. "But that's where many people meet their future partners..."

"Don't tell Dad, whatever you do," I said. "He'll give me the third degree about him. We're just friendly right now so there's no reason to get him all interested, okay?"

She didn't say anything, and I realized it was ridiculous to expect her to keep quiet about something as momentous as me having a new BF.

"At least promise me that you'll wait to tell him about Keith until you go back to Concord. Okay? I don't need him pestering me for information, considering that nothing may come of it."

"Your father will just want to make sure that you're okay, dear," my mother said. "But I'll wait if you really want me to."

I nodded. "I do, I do," I said, trying to drive home to her how much I did. "Please wait until you're on the flight back. At least then the most he can do is call me on the phone or text me."

She shook her head. "I don't know why you'd want to keep it from your poor father."

I sighed. There was no use arguing with her. Jerkface had a good pedigree and while he wasn't as wealthy as Josh, he had an inheritance. He went to an Ivy League school, worked for a top political law firm who did work for my father. My mother would be calculating how much less money someone like 'Keith' would make than Jerkface.

I knew it.

If she knew about Josh, she'd be ecstatic, but if my father knew about Josh, he'd be infuriated.

I was caught between the proverbial rock and hard place.

If anything more developed between us, I'd come clean about Josh but until then, I figured it was a better idea to keep them in the dark about my own Mr. Big.

No sense in creating a bunch of drama over nothing.

WE MET MY FATHER FOR DINNER SUNDAY NIGHT AND HAD a nice time, until the time came for my father to ask about my social life.

"She met a young man," my mother said, totally forgetting I had asked her to keep quiet about it.

"Mother!"

My father turned to me, his eyes widening.

Oh, oh...

"When were you going to tell me?" he asked, wiping his mouth and sitting back in his chair. "You met some new man? Who is it?"

He turned to my mother and she just shrugged. "I wasn't supposed to say anything. You'll have to ask your daughter."

He turned back to me. "Well?"

"Well, what?" I said, frustrated, giving my mother the stink eye.

"Tell me about this young man. What's his name? What do you know about his family?"

"He's a bicycle courier," my mother said, and then she covered her mouth like it just slipped out.

The expression on my father's face was almost laughable except I was afraid of that expression because it meant I'd be pestered and pestered about him.

"He's working as a bicycle courier as he goes to college to get his degree in Commerce," I said, upset now that I had to defend a fictitious Keith, blending the story I first thought about Josh with the truth about his past. "He wants to be an entrepreneur when he graduates."

My father turned back to his food and cut his steak, and I could see the wheels turning in his mind. He was struggling to figure out how to respond, knowing that his instinct was to be dismissive, but fighting it in an attempt to appear reasonable.

"What do you know about his family? What's his last name?" he asked.

"If you think I'm telling you, you're crazy," I said and took a long drink of my wine. "We just met and are just friendly. We went out for a meal and have gone to a bar with other employees from work. If anything more develops, I'll let you know."

"Okay, dear, whatever you think is best," he replied, and I was surprised that he was so willing to accede to my wishes. "If and when you want to let us know more, you can always call me, and I'll come down and meet him or you two could come up to Concord for the Christmas or New Year's holidays. Keep it in mind."

"I will, Daddy," I said and smiled. "Thanks for understanding."

. . .

THE DINNER ENDED AND SO I WENT BACK TO MY TINY studio apartment and went to bed, waiting for Josh to call me so we could talk -- and maybe Skype sex if he was interested. Frankly, I was tired from my day walking around Manhattan with my mother and could have happily just talked with Josh, but I knew that if I heard that sexy voice and watched him, my body would respond, and I'd be ready and eager.

My cell dinged, indicating an incoming text.

JOSH: How was your day?

I smiled when I saw his text and sent a reply.

ELLA: Good. I had lunch with my mom and made the mistake of telling her about losing my ID and stuff. I said a nice bicycle courier helped me out and of course, I got grilled about you for the rest of the day. I didn't say who you really were, though. I don't need the aggravation.

JOSH: That's too bad. I'd like to meet your father.

ELLA: I don't think you would like to meet him. He thinks you're the enemy.

JOSH: That's no good. I don't want to be anyone's enemy. Especially not your father...

ELLA: It's the bad blood between them because of what happened to my father's business partner.

JOSH: I understand. They were friends as well as partners. He took it personally, I guess.

ELLA: Yes, and he still holds a grudge against MBC because of it. What's going on in La-La-Land? Are you having fun?

JOSH: They're working on music for a new EP at David's villa, so the place has been busy as you can imagine a rocker's villa would be.

ELLA: Lots of pretty young thangs? Groupies dying to be with the boys from the band? Should I be jealous?

JOSH: No, not in the least. There are a few women around, but believe it or not, they're actually girlfriends or wives of the band members. No groupies in sight. You'd think the guys were all hard rockers because of the music, but they're mostly just musicians and family men or in serious relationships. All except David, that is. He's a confirmed bachelor.

ELLA: In my father's parlance, that means he's gay.

JOSH: Nope. Just really sour on marriage. He's in between girlfriends but he makes it pretty clear he's not interested in anything monogamous.

ELLA: I guess he can get away with it. So, are you enjoying your stay?

JOSH: It's nice in SOCAL but I wish you were here with me. I'm going to Skype you, so I can hear your voice and see your face.

ELLA: Okay.

In a moment, my cell rang, and I answered it, positioning the phone so he could see my face.

"So, how is it being at David's?"

"Fun, as you can imagine a rock star's mansion would be."

"They're recording an EP, right?"

"They are but he's pretty under control when they're recording, so I'll be able to get work done."

"That's good," I said, smiling, happy that even if we weren't together, at least I could see his face and hear his voice. "Are you excited about the coming week, and the new office?

"I am. I'm thinking of seeing if I could get a paper going on this coast. That way, I'd have both coasts covered."

"You're ambitious," I said with a laugh. "In an age when

digital is taking up such a huge chunk of the market, that's going against the grain."

"I have a feeling people are going to continue to read actual print papers, but I would definitely have a digital side. Can't fight progress. We'll see."

We talked for another hour back and forth and frankly, I was glad that Josh didn't bring up a sext session. It was enough to just talk to him.

When I couldn't stifle a yawn and he saw me try, he laughed. "I can see I'm keeping you up. We'll try again tomorrow night and I promise to call you sooner."

"I'm sorry," I said and pouted. "I'm just beat from all the walking and talking. I guess I should take up some kind of sport and get in better shape."

"You could get a bike and ride every day like me."

"Oh, God, I'd be afraid I'd be hit by a car. Manhattan is a lot different from the roads of Concord..."

"You could take side streets to the bike path along the Hudson and you'd be fine."

"I'll think about it."

"Good night, Ella," he said with a soft smile.

"Good night, Josh," I said and blew him a kiss.

He mimed catching it and then signed off. I put my phone away and leaned back, glad that he'd Skyped me, so we could see each other.

I fell asleep almost instantly and didn't wake again until a full seven hours later.

I SPENT MONDAY WITH MY MOM, DOING MOSTLY TOURISTY things. We went to the Museum of Natural History and walked through the exhibits, got some street meat at a vendor parked under a bridge, and then went to the Metropolitan Museum of Art and checked out the collections.

Finally, when we were both exhausted, we went to the spa in the hotel and had a massage, pedicure and manicure and met my father for dinner at a restaurant he'd heard about near their hotel.

While I waited for my mom, I got a text from Josh.

JOSH: *Wish you were here. The weather is fine, and the sky is crystal clear.*

I responded right away, smiling to myself. I had to keep reminding myself that LA was several hours earlier than Manhattan.

ELLA: *I wish I was there, too, but I am having a nice visit with the parental units.*

JOSH: *Enjoy them while you can. I wish I could do the same.*

ELLA: *I will, and I do. What's on your agenda for the rest of the week?*

JOSH: *Probably spend my time during the day at the office and then spend time with David at night.*

ELLA: *You should go surfing or something.*

JOSH: *I might hit up my brother between recording sessions. He surfs on occasion so he might be up for it.*

ELLA: *Wish I was there, too.*

I said goodbye and wished I was there, but at the same time, I valued my time with my parents.

THE CAPITAL GRILL WAS AN UPSCALE CHOP HOUSE WITH delicious food and a high four-star rating. It was a nice end to a very busy day. The talk was about my father's meetings with his political cronies about the upcoming by-election, and he and my mom did the whole inside baseball talk about who was who and everything I used to care about but no longer did.

When I was with Jerkface, that world was mine as well, but after we split, I was no longer so connected into all the political talk. I was just as glad to be free of it, frankly. I knew it was important, but at the same time, I was now jaded. I'd been burned and while I knew my father was an honorable man, I had a bad taste in my mouth after my experience of Jerkface being so politically ambitious, he would try to marry me to get an in with my father.

As a result, I didn't want to even talk politics.

"We're boring you, dear," my father said, when I hid my yawn behind a hand.

"Sorry, Dad," I replied and gave him a guilty smile. "I used to be interested, but I'm kind of out of the loop."

"Politics is too important to leave to other people," he said, softly chiding me. "I thought you understood that."

"I do," I protested. "I vote, and I always know the local issues. You know me. But I'm just not that interested in New Hampshire any longer. I feel like I have to learn New York politics, if anything."

"Good God, don't say that," he said with a huge laugh. "One of the most corrupt states in the Union. Mafia bosses control pretty much everything."

"Daddy," I said, frowning. "It's not like that."

My mother must have kicked him under the table because he grunted and shot her a withering look.

"You'll find out for yourself, I guess," he said and focused on his dessert.

"She will find out for herself, won't you, Dear?" my mother replied, smiling to dissipate the tension.

"I will."

"That's settled," my father replied and motioned to the waiter for the check. "Let's go for a stroll. I've been inside all day and would like to see the sights."

After he paid the check, we got our coats and walked along 42nd Street, past the Chrysler Building, one of the most iconic buildings in Manhattan. We went to Bryant Park and then up Madison Avenue to the Ritz-Carlton.

It was nice to walk along Madison Avenue at night, exciting, and exactly what I thought of when I dreamed of moving to Manhattan.

Finally, I said goodnight to them both and took a taxi to my apartment, pleased with how the day had gone and glad that I wasn't grilled about the bicycle courier I mentioned the day before. They were leaving when my father's final meeting was over, so I would see them both for lunch and then say our goodbyes.

I couldn't wait to get home and spend some time with the bicycle-courier in question.

6
JOSH

Since I wasn't going into the office until Wednesday, Tuesday was one of those lazy days in LA when the sun was warm, the sky blue and I had nothing to do but lie around, read newspapers and think about what I'd rather be doing.

Namely, Ella.

While I was sitting beside the pool, I got a text from Penny.

PENNY: *My email is pennyMC92@gmail.com.*

I realized that meant she was asking for some money. Had she already spent the hundred bucks?

Knowing junkies, she probably bought herself a lot of heroin and a tiny bit of food and had spent the last two days high.

Probably got her friends high as well.

I sent another hundred to her via an email transfer. If I really wanted to help her, I had to find her a rehab place. Maybe if she had it all paid, she'd go and get sober. Then, I could really help her. Find a job, get a decent place to live.

It was the least I could do to honor Grant's memory. How sad he must have been to see her like that. She was a party girl when I met her three years earlier, but I never got the sense that she would become an addict.

DAVID'S VILLA BECAME EXACTLY WHAT I EXPECTED A rocker's villa to be like -- beautiful women in skimpy bathing suits, lying around the pool, music playing in the background as the band practiced.

Luckily, the beautiful women were all wives and girl-friends and so they left me alone. I could appreciate a beautiful woman, but after having been burned by a cheating fiancée, I had no interest in even encouraging a woman other than Ella to pay me any attention.

Whereas I might have welcomed some light flirting before, now that I was with Ella, I didn't want anything to happen that would either make me feel guilty or make me imagine the same thing happening to her. I was, at base, a monogamous guy.

My father had been monogamous, had always encouraged us to be honorable with women and treat them as equals, and he'd clearly been deeply in love with my mother. She was an amazing woman and accomplished for her generation with a degree in politics, and who did political consulting.

He never remarried after she died and focused instead of his large brood of sons. The brothers and I expected him to live a long time after she died, and for him to remarry, but unfortunately, that wasn't the case.

Theirs was the kind of relationship I wanted as well.

David sat beside me. "Soaking up the sun?" he said and pulled his sunglasses lower to glance at me. I was in trunks and had to admit I looked like a ghost compared to his tanned and tatted bare chest.

"Hey, do you know of any good rehab places? One that does the wholistic approach to getting someone sober and back into society?"

He frowned. "Sure," he said. "There are a few great places in the hills. A few people in the industry I know have gone to this one place called Cedars Second Chances. You have someone who needs rehab?"

"An old buddy's sister," I said. Then I told David about Grant's death.

"Oh, man, that's rough," he said and reach over to squeeze my arm. "If you want, I can get you the number. You gonna try to help her?"

"If she's ready for help."

He nodded. "You have to be ready or else it's a waste of time."

David got up and glanced around. "Well, I have to go back in. Record some more tracks. Are you okay out here by yourself?"

"I'm a big boy."

"Put some sunscreen on or you'll be a very burnt boy. You look like a ghost."

I laughed and took the sunscreen tube from him.

"Yes, little brother."

He cracked a smile and then left me by the pool.

AN HOUR OR SO LATER, AS I LAY IN THE SHADE AND DRANK a fresh coffee, David came back out of the house and flopped down on the lawn chair beside me.

"What's up?" I asked, putting down my paper. "You finished recording?"

"For the time being."

"What's on the rest of your rock star agenda for the day?"

"Mitch is a bit under the weather today with a cold. Wanna get the hell out of here?" David asked. "I feel like I've been holed up practicing for too long."

"Sure," I said. "I have today off, so whatever you feel like. What about surfing?"

"Yeah!" he said and sat up, looking excited. "I haven't been surfing for ages. I'll probably fall off the board and break my neck and there goes the EP, but what the hell. Terry will probably want to come, too. He's a really good surfer and the swells are really good this time of year."

I shook my head. "We don't have to, if you're not up to it. I can amuse myself if you think surfing is too dangerous for you."

"Oh, I'm up to it. I have to be safe about it though. I'm insured but I don't want to delay the EP in case anything happened."

"We could boogie board instead," I said with a laugh.

"We could at that," he chuckled. "Probably more my speed."

"Nah," I said and we both laughed.

So, while the band took a couple hours off from practicing, David and I and one of his band mates, Terry, went to Venice Beach and did some surfing.

"Venice Beach has pretty mellow waves," Terry said, who was the expert surfer among the three of us.

"That's exactly what we're looking for," I said.

"That's exactly as much as the two of us can handle," David said with a laugh. "It's been at least a year since I went surfing."

"Me, too," I replied. The last time I went surfing had been on a trip to visit David when I was still with Christie.

DAVID DROVE US TO VENICE BEACH IN HIS SLICK NEW BMW SUV. For the next two hours, from three o'clock until five, we spent our time in the waves off Venice Beach, and I noted that David still put his all into it, despite claiming he didn't want to risk hurting himself. He was a good surfer, much better than me, but he'd spent the last eight years in LA and had more time to improve.

As the big brother, I tried my best to compete with him, but each of us had our own talents. Surfing was not my best sport.

"That was a magnificent wipe out," David said to me after a spectacular fall I took while trying a wave that was perhaps a bit too big for me.

"It was. I think I won the competition for today."

"You did," David said with a laugh. "I'll grant you that."

"I think that deserves at least a beer," Terry said and so the three of us returned the surfboards to the rental company, packed up and walked along the boardwalk, enjoying the sights.

We came to a restaurant along the boardwalk that served fish tacos and cold imported beer and decided to make a meal out of it. We sat for about an hour, eating and talking business, the band, the Chronicle, and our plans for the future.

"Have another beer," David said. "Let's celebrate."

"We have to drive back," I replied.

"I'll drive," Terry said. "You two brothers have another beer. Enjoy yourselves."

"Thanks, bro," David said and ordered us another beer.

Finally, at about six thirty, we piled back into the car, with Terry at the helm, and drove back to Brentwood.

Only, we didn't make it.

COMING AROUND A SHARP CORNER ON SUNSET Boulevard near Rustic Creek, we hit another vehicle head-on that wandered into our lane. It happened so fast, there wasn't really any time to avoid the car and while we weren't traveling too fast, it sounded like two freight trains hitting as our front end mashed into the front end of the BMW.

While it took only seconds, it seemed to take forever for the cars to stop skidding along the road before we stopped. After we hit the BMW, our vehicle slid into the embankment, the SUV flipping over onto its roof. The other vehicle crashed into the trees on the side of the street.

For the first ten seconds, I blinked, trying to figure out what to do, but then my survival instincts kicked in. I wasn't hurt too badly. I was hanging upside down, but the air bags had deployed and since I was in the back seat on the far side from the driver, who took the brunt of the hit, I was fine.

"Are you guys okay?" I called out to David and Terry.

There was no answer at first, and I struggled to unlatch my seatbelt. I finally managed it, bracing myself with one arm so that I didn't injure myself when I fell from the seat onto the crumpled roof.

A car had stopped on the side of the road and as I tried to kick open the side door, I saw the driver get out and take out his cell. I assumed he was calling 9-1-1 but the safety app on the SUV's dashboard had already done so.

The front of the roof was really crumpled. I managed to crawl out and after I checked myself out, I tried to get the passenger door open. David was still hanging upside down and wasn't moving. I didn't hear anything from either of them, and from what I could see, Terry's side of the vehicle was pretty mangled.

I didn't think. I just did.

The engine was smoking, and I was afraid it would catch fire so although I was worried about removing David before I knew whether he had a back or neck injury, I didn't want him to burn alive in case the fire spread.

I finally managed to get the passenger door opened and the man who called 9-1-1 helped me to get David out. He had a gash in the side of his head, but I couldn't tell if anything else was broken. We laid him on the ground a dozen feet away on the grass, and I listened to his heart, which was slow and steady. He was alive, and he was breathing, but he was still unconscious. I took off my shirt and t-shirt, so I could use the t-shirt to bandage David's head, then I hands down David's arms and legs, checking for broken bones and any cuts. Thankfully, there didn't appear to be any.

Another car stopped, and someone ran to the other vehicle that hit us. It was pretty badly banged up and I hoped that whoever it was, they were okay, but they had a BMW and it wasn't as sturdy as our SUV. The good Samaritan who was helping us was named Don. He went back to his vehicle and grabbed a fire extinguisher from his trunk, which he used on the engine to extinguish the flames that were sprouting from interior. Then he went to check on Terry. A third car had stopped, and the driver was helping him check out the car to see if they could reach him, but the vehicle was wedged on its roof against the side of a hill.

I slipped my shirt back on and held a corner of my t-shirt to David's cut over his right eye. Finally, David's eyes blinked open.

"What the hell..."

I wiped some blood out of his right eye.

"We were in an accident," I said, keeping my voice calm. "You've got a cut over your eye, but you don't appear to have any broken bones."

A siren wailed in the distance and I knew that a rescue unit was on the way.

"What about Terry?" David managed, grimacing in pain.

"They're trying to get him out," I said. "The firefighters will be able to deal with it and they're on their way. You just focus on yourself, okay?"

"Okay," he said and tried to move his head.

"Don't move," I said and held his shoulders. "Just stay still until the EMTs arrive."

"Okay," he said, his voice weak. "Is Terry okay?"

"Don't worry about Terry," I said, because I really couldn't tell if Terry was even alive. He was trapped inside the crumpled front driver's side, wedged against the embankment. I hadn't heard him say anything, so I assumed he was unconscious. He bore the brunt of the accident, and his side of the vehicle was the most damaged. "The ambulance is coming. Just relax. Focus on me."

The first vehicle to arrive was a firetruck. Out jumped two firefighters, who brought over a case that contained their life-saving equipment. One came over and checked out David, while the second firefighter joined the other men, who were trying to reach Terry.

An ambulance arrived on scene and the two EMTs took over from the firefighter, who gave them some basic stats for David. They put on a neck brace, and got David up on a gurney, then slid him into an ambulance. I went with him in the back of the ambulance and sat on the jump seat beside the EMT while he checked David's vitals and dealt with the wound over his eye. On my way into the ambulance, I saw that they had taken a person out of the other car and had lain him on the ground and were administering CPR. It didn't look good, whoever he was. There was another passenger as well -- a woman with long black hair, a neck brace on, her face bloodied.

At least she appeared to be alive by the way the EMT was treating her.

WE ARRIVED AT THE EMERGENCY ROOM OF UCLA SANTA Monica. The transition from the ambulance to the ER was smooth. I went inside the examination room with David, watching as they worked on him, assessing him for any broken bones and attaching ECG monitors to his chest so they could watch his stats. They took his blood pressure and measured his oxygen. A doc came in the room and did a neurological exam, then they took David for diagnostic imaging to check for any internal injuries. I waited in the examination room, then finally, alone, I checked my messages.

I expected to see one from Ella, but there wasn't anything. I checked my watch -- it would be nearly midnight back home.

I texted her to let her know I was okay.

JOSH: Sorry I haven't contacted you, but we were in a bad accident on Sunset Blvd and I'm at the hospital with David.

Her response was immediate.

ELLA: Oh, Josh -- are you okay? What happened? Is David all right?

JOSH: He's getting a CT scan right now. I think he's okay, but they're checking for internal injuries. I think David's band mate, Terry, is pretty bad. They were still trying to get him out of the SUV when we left for the ER.

ELLA: I'm so sorry. I was wondering what happened that you hadn't texted me, but I figured you were just out too late. I'll be thinking of David and your other friend.

JOSH: Thanks. I think David will be all right, physically. He doesn't appear to have broken bones, but you never know what's going on inside. I'll let you know how things are in the morning.

ELLA: I wish I was with you, so I could keep you company. It must be nerve wracking to be waiting to find out how he is.

JOSH: I wish you were here, too. It's Terry I'm more worried about.

ELLA: Oh, God, I hope he's okay...

JOSH: I realize it's really late there and you have to work tomorrow so I'll sign off for now and will text you in the a.m.

ELLA: Good night, Josh. *Hugs*

JOSH: Good night, Ella. *Hugs you back*

I felt a little better after texting with Ella but was worried when David still hadn't come back to the observation room in the ER half an hour later.

Finally, a nurse came over to me. "Mr. Macintyre, your brother was taken into surgery from the radiology department because they discovered internal bleeding and needed to do emergency surgery. I'll let you know more when we have any updates. There's a lounge with some recliners down the hall, in case you want to sleep."

I thanked the nurse and went to the hallway, finding a dim room with four recliners, each walled off by a sheet from the others. I took one recliner and spread the blanket over me, glad to have the place to myself.

My only hope was that when I woke, the news I got would be that David had come through surgery well and was in recovery.

I closed my eyes and tried to blank my mind, but sleep was a long time in coming. With Grant's recent suicide and now this accident, my emotions were all over the place. I realized that I had to get control over myself, so I could be there for David.

He needed me to be strong, so I pushed my sadness into a corner of my mind and tried think only about how to help my brother recover.

7
ELLA

When I woke Wednesday morning, I saw a new text from Josh that he'd sent sometime during the night.

JOSH: David had emergency surgery due to internal injuries. I don't know what exactly they did but I'll let you know as soon as I find out. David's friend Terry is in critical condition. Not sure if he will survive the night. I'm sleeping in the hospital lounge on a recliner, with one of those hospital blankets on me. Talk later.

I sent a text right away.

ELLA: I'm so sorry about David needing surgery and about his friend Terry. How terrible. Let me know when you hear more.

I didn't hear back right away, so I assumed he was sleeping. It was only four a.m., in California.

It was terrible, but I was so glad Josh was fine. Relieved but at the same time, it sounded like the crash was bad enough that their friend Terry might not make it. I felt a sense of doom at the thought of how fragile we all were and that at any minute, it could all change. I was a nervous driver at the best of times, preferring public transit to private cars, and this just made me even happier to be in Manhattan and using the subway and busses instead of driving. I was even nervous in taxi cabs, but you had to take them sometimes.

I finished getting ready for work and then left my apartment, glancing around it one last time before I left. I was so lucky to be living in Chelsea in this tiny studio, with a sexy and very handsome new boyfriend, with a job I dreamed of.

The accident and the danger David's friend was in made me appreciate it even more.

WORK WAS BUSY, AND I MET WITH SHARON TO DISCUSS some of the books I'd selected for review the previous week. My father and mother were going to pop up later to see me for lunch. My father insisted he wanted to see my office -- probably not really believing I had a job and an office and was really working, so I agreed. I'd show them around, introduce them to Sharon and then we'd go out.

When noon rolled around, I tidied up my desk in wait for them to arrive. Sure enough, at just after twelve o'clock, I got a call from the front desk that a nice couple was waiting for me, claiming to be my parents.

I went down to the main floor to meet them, and together, we rode up in the elevator. On the way up, the elevator stopped and on got Keith, who I had used as my stand-in for Josh when talking about meeting someone and dating. I used Keith's name just to shut my mother up, never thinking that they'd ever actually get to or want to meet him.

I cringed internally, regretting that I ever mentioned his name to my parents, but that was my life.

"Hey, Ella," Keith said and smiled. He glanced over my parents and I knew that he recognized my dad immediately. He probably already knew my story and so recognized my father. He was a hard man to forget with his eagle nose and salt-and-pepper hair.

"Hi," I said and felt my cheeks heat immediately.

"Governor Carlson," Keith said and extended his hand. "Nice to meet you, Sir. Keith Johnson." They shook, and I saw that my father was pleased to be recognized in Manhattan of all places.

"Good to meet you, young man. This is my wife, Mary."

They gave each other a smile.

"Ella's told us all about you," she said. "You're the bicycle courier she ran into on her first day at work, if I recall the story correctly. Isn't that right, Ella?" she asked and turned to me, smiling, her eyes wide and pleased. "This is the Keith you mentioned? I thought he was a bicycle courier."

"She told you about how we met, did she?" Keith said and gave me a knowing smile. "I really want to work in publishing, so being a courier is just a side gig."

He winked at me. He must have figured out that I told my parents that I was dating him instead of Josh, not wanting them to know the truth.

Oh, God.

I half-wished that the elevator floor would open up and I could fall to the bottom of the shaft and end my misery, but he didn't say anything else and played along. He stepped closer to me and made some joke about my first day in Manhattan -- he obviously knew the story of how Josh and I almost ran into each other that first day and recounted it.

"And that's how we met," Keith said and looked down at me with mock affection. "A minor disaster that turned out to be one of the best days of my life so far."

He laughed, and my father did as well, but I could tell by my father's expression that he was assessing Keith carefully. Keith got off on his floor and before the doors closed, he turned before they did. "Nice to meet you. I'd offer to take you all out for a drink, but I've got late deliveries so maybe another time."

"Nice to meet you, Keith," my mother said and gave him a huge smile.

Finally, the elevator doors closed and my parents both turned to me.

"He seems like a nice young man," my mother said.

"Good manners," my father added.

"He's very nice."

We arrived on our floor a few moments later and I was never so glad to get off the elevator. After introducing them to everyone we passed in the hallway, I took them to my office. My father was suitably impressed.

"Good view," he said, peering down at the back alley far below my window.

"You can see for miles," I said and pointed out the Manhattan skyline.

"It's beautiful, dear," my mother said. "We're so proud of you, aren't we?"

She nudged my father with her elbow -- a move that wasn't lost on me.

"Oh, yes, of course we are," my father said. "I'm glad I met

Keith. He wasn't dressed like a bicycle courier. You never told us he wanted to work in publishing."

"The company has an apartment and so he changes his clothes in it before he goes on a delivery run," I said, ad-libbing, hoping they didn't push to have dinner with him. I waved my hand. "Besides, we're just casually dating. Nothing serious."

My mother raised her eyebrows at that, and of course, I knew what she was thinking -- she was thinking my father would take that to mean 'casual sex', which was not at all what I meant.

"At least, we're not serious yet. We're both busy with work and going to be going to school next year, hopefully."

I smiled, hoping my father didn't push.

"I don't know if--" My father started to speak but my mother elbowed him, and he stopped. He actually turned to her and frowned, but she smiled at me like nothing happened.

"We'll spend time with him when you want us to, dear," she said. "We won't poke our noses into your private life."

"Thanks for understanding," I said. "We just started to see each other and so nothing's settled."

I didn't like to lie, but I also didn't want my father to know I was dating Josh. The very last thing I wanted was for Josh to feel like my father was going to judge him because of Joshua Sr's Actions decades ago. While I felt weak-kneed about Josh and knew I wanted to be with him, I had no idea what our future entailed.

I took them in to meet Sharon, and they were pleased when Sharon told them how happy she was to have me working for her.

"Ella saved my life," she said, her hand over her heart. "I'm serious. I had no editorial assistant for two weeks and the manuscripts were piling up. I was afraid I'd have nothing to show for our big editorial meeting, but Ella came through and found us some really promising books."

Sharon turned to me and smiled, and it made me really happy that I was actually appreciated. I didn't mind the long hours when she was so positive about my performance.

"Maybe you could pay her one of these days," my father said, rather gruffly. He was smiling, but his tone was disapproving.

Sharon didn't bite at my father's bait. "Absolutely. I hope she'll stay on part-time when her internship is over and work for us as a permanent employee once she's done her Master's."

"I don't know why she wants to do her Master's degree," my father said. "Seems she could do the job without it."

"Daddy," I said, gently chiding him. "I want to get an MFA so I can teach one day if I want to. I want to write. You know that."

"I do, but it seems you're doing a good job as an editorial assistant. You could be an editor one day. Do you need an MA for that?" he asked Sharon.

She shook her head. "No, she doesn't, but it wouldn't hurt. I'm sure you can understand that credentials help when we're picking employees. If she has an MA, especially if she has editing experience, I expect she could get a job working for any publishing house."

My father nodded as if that satisfied him. He really didn't think I should go and do my MA. I was surprised but I expect he thought I should have been married to his former attorney instead of dating a bicycle courier and working for free.

Yes, he'd fired Jerkface, but I knew he really still wished we were together. Maybe even that I should forgive him his indiscretion.

Not on your life.

"Did you hear that Josh was in an accident and his brother was injured?" Sharon said before we left her office. Of course, I felt extremely awkward about her mentioning Josh. My father's ears pricked up at the mention of his name.

"Really?" I said, trying to sound surprised. "That's terrible."

"Yes, it is. We're lucky that Josh wasn't injured. Just a bit scraped up but he's fine. His brother broke some bones. I guess their friend is not going to make it." She shook her head and clucked her tongue.

"Joshua Macintyre?" my father said, stepping closer to Sharon's desk.

"Yes," Sharon said. "Do you know him?"

"I knew his father," my father replied dryly.

"Were you friends? You must have been surprised to learn of his death."

"Not really friends," my father said, and his tone indicated he didn't feel bad at all. "His news station did some hit pieces on my business partner years back. We had a history, shall we say." He raised his eyebrows suggestively.

I could tell Sharon got the picture that my father didn't like Joshua Macintyre Sr.

She nodded and smiled nervously.

"Nice to meet you," my mother said, pulling my father away. "I'm glad to know Ella is doing well as an editorial assistant. She was really excited to get the position." She gave Sharon a big smile.

"Nice to meet you, too," Sharon said.

I managed to push my parents out of Sharon's office and

gave her a meaningful look as I closed her door. "I'll talk to you later."

She nodded, and I herded my parents back to the elevator, glad that we had to leave for our lunch date.

"Have you met Macintyre?" my father asked, turning to me, his arms crossed. I could tell he was spoiling for a fight at the mere thought I worked for his arch nemesis's son.

"Yes, but he's now the CEO of MBC and he doesn't have much to do with publishing. He hired someone to manage it for him from what I understand. Last I heard was that he bought *The Chronicle* and is trying to revitalize it."

"What's he like, dear?" my mother asked. "He's handsome, from his picture. His father was quite the looker when he was younger."

"He's attractive, I guess," I said in as nonchalant a way as I could manage.

"He's ex-Army, or so I read," my father said, adjusting his tie and checking himself out in the reflection in the mirrored walls of the elevator.

"Really?" I said, pretending that I had no idea about Josh's past.

My mother reached over and laid her hand on my arm. "Next time we're in town, we'll have to get together with you and Keith. Have dinner together."

"If we're still seeing each other," I said with a nervous laugh.

"He's cute," she replied and gave me a wink. "I'm glad to see that you're making new friends. I was afraid you'd be lonely all by yourself, what with Steph staying in Concord and you and Derek breaking up. You're on the rebound, so keep that in mind when you're dating." She nodded meaningfully.

"I know, Mom," I said and gave her arm a squeeze. "I'll be extra careful not to get involved with anyone too soon."

"Speaking of Derek," my mother said, her eyes wide. "Did you know that he broke up with that piece of trash he had the affair with? Bambi or whatever her name was?"

"Bunni," I said derisively. "With an 'i'."

"Yes, that's right. Bunni with an 'i'. Honestly, I can't believe how bad women are to fellow members of our sex."

"I can't believe how members of the opposite sex cheat on the women they claim to love," I said with a shrug. Although I didn't love Jerkface anymore, the betrayal still stung. I don't think there could be a worse form of betrayal than by the man or woman you thought loved you and were planning on marrying.

At least Josh and I had *that* in common...

"Both sexes cheat," my father said derisively. "It takes two to tango..."

"It does," I replied and finally, we arrived on the main floor and left the building.

I was so glad to be out of Macintyre Publishing, hoping I didn't run into Keith again or be forced to lie any more than I already had to my parents.

I loved them, but I would be glad when they returned to New Hampshire. Soon enough, I'd have to come clean about dating Josh, but I didn't want to get into it until I had a better idea whether we would stay together.

I wanted to -- I felt giddy whenever I thought about him, but I'd been burned and too recently to have much faith.

I hoped Josh proved me wrong.

8

JOSH

After David returned from the OR and was settled into his observation room, I spent the night in the lounge outside the ICU. Sleep was fitful, and I was awoken several times as people entered or left the ward. In the morning when I woke for the final time, I checked on David. It was around seven in the morning and hospital kitchen workers were pushing around the meal carts for breakfast. David was gone from his room and for a moment, I panicked, thinking that he'd gotten worse while I slept and was back in surgery.

I rushed to the nursing station and bent over the counter, frantic to know where he was.

"Can you tell me where David Macintyre is? He's not in his room."

The nurse glanced up from her monitor. "Mr. Macintyre is getting another MRI to check on his injuries. He should be back pretty soon." She gave me a smile and I relaxed a bit.

I wiped my brow dramatically. "For a moment, I was worried that he went back into surgery or something."

"No, it's just a follow-up scan to make sure he is okay to be moved to the surgical ward. You should be able to take see him once he's back and the doctors have done morning rounds."

I went back to the lounge and fixed myself a cup of coffee and a piece of toast with peanut butter, graciously provided for family members who were spending time in the lounge. Then, I waited.

While I waited, I sent an email to one of the security techs at MBC who often did research for the paper to get background on people for news articles.

JOSH: *Hey Pete, can you do a full background check on this old friend of mine? Her name is Penelope McNeil and she's from Millbrook, Alabama. She's currently a junkie and I'm hoping to help her get into rehab.*

PETE: *Sure thing, boss. You want a full background? I can talk to local police to see if she has a record, that sort of thing.*

JOSH: *Whatever you can find out. I appreciate it. She's the sister of an old army buddy who recently died and she's not doing well.*

PETE: *No prob. I understand.*

For the next hour, I read over the headlines on my cell, trying to get caught back up with the world after the previous day spent surfing and then in the hospital. I checked my watch and at around nine, I went back to the nursing station.

"He's still not back in his room," I said, starting to get worried.

"Oh, Mr. Macintyre was taken to the ward already. I'm sorry but you must have been in the washroom when it happened, and I didn't see you to tell you. You should be able to go up now."

I thanked her and took the elevator up to the surgical ward, stopping in to ask the nurses there how he was.

"He's a bit sleepy but he's stable. The docs are doing rounds right now so if you'd like, you can wait in the family lounge just down the hall. They should be done in fifteen minutes."

When the time had finally come that I could visit David, I went into his room just as his nurse was finishing recording his vitals. She gave me a smile and I went over to David's side. His eyes were closed so I assumed he was sleeping. I didn't want to wake him but was glad to see that he was still breathing, and his color was a bit better than the last time I saw him.

I pulled a chair over beside the bed and sat down, taking out my cell so I could read more news headlines while he slept.

He must have heard the chair scrape along the floor for he woke up, his eyes cracking open.

"There you are," he said, his voice soft.

"How are you, little brother?" I asked and bent down, kissing him on the forehead. "You gave me quite the scare."

"What's with all the kissing?" he said and smiled, although his eyes were closed. "You haven't kissed me since you were drunk after you called off your engagement."

"I'm all emotional that you're still alive, that's what's with all the kissing," I said with a chuckle. He was only teasing for if anyone was an overly affectionate type, it was David, who was always hugging and kissing everyone else.

He sighed. "Terry died in the night," he said, his voice sounding tired. "They were waiting to tell me until the results came back from my MRI. I guess they didn't want to upset me or something."

"I'm so sorry," I said and felt a stab of regret in my gut.

95

Terry was a great guy. I only knew him from that visit, but he was friendly and seemed a really good friend of David's.

"At least he donated his organs, so something good will come of this."

"How did he die?"

"Brain injury," David said. He sighed and then he lifted his hand up and covered his eyes, holding back a sob. I reached out and squeezed his arm, wanting to comfort him. "He had two little kids."

"I'm sorry."

Life was so fragile. One minute you were alive. The next, you weren't. It seemed so trite, but it was shocking when you realized it up close and personally.

Having just lost Grant, I knew how David was feeling.

I leaned down and kissed him again, holding onto his shoulder gently, trying to give him some kind of comfort, but I knew there was nothing I could really do to ease his pain.

There just wasn't. Losing someone who had once been close to me, I knew that all too well.

I LEFT DAVID TO SLEEP FOR A WHILE AFTER HE'D regained his composure. While I waited, I called the family back East to let them know about David. I didn't want to send them a text until I knew whether David would survive, but now that I felt pretty secure that he was going to recover, I had to let them know.

The brothers and I did a conference call and I was able to speak with each one and with each other.

"I'll probably stay here until David gets discharged and I

know he has all the care he needs in place. Maybe a week at least," I said.

"Do you want any of us to come and give you a hand?" Christian asked.

"Not necessary unless you really want to come. I have things handled, but if you have the time, feel free."

"I might pop out there just for a few days, to help out," Christian said. "I'm not teaching this semester, so I have the time."

"I'll pick you up at the airport. Let me know when your flight arrives."

We said our goodbyes and I ended the conference call, glad that Christian was coming. He was pretty reliable as brothers went. Very serious, studious, a straight arrow-type.

I knew he'd be a comfort to David during his recovery.

WHILE DAVID RECOVERED QUICKLY OVER THE NEXT couple of days, I alternated my time between the new office of MBC and the hospital. When the day came to discharge David, Christian arrived and the two of us brought David home to his mansion in the hills.

He had a big incision in is belly, and so he had a few weeks of recovery ahead of him. What most upset him was that he would have to miss Terry's funeral. There was no way David could go, given how soon after surgery it was.

"I feel so bad," David said to us and Christian and I helped him get settled onto the sofa in his living room. "I should be at the funeral."

"Don't feel that way," Christian replied. "You got out of

emergency surgery on a couple of days ago and need to heal. Nothing strenuous for six weeks."

David laid back on the sofa and allowed me to pull a blanket over him while Christian got him a cup of coffee.

"I'm going to the new office for the rest of the afternoon, but Christian will be with you in case you need anything," I said to David as I brought over the newspaper for him to read.

"Thanks," David said and closed his eyes. "Even just the trip home has tired me out. I think I'll have a little nap."

I squeezed his shoulder and patted Christian on the back. "Call me if you need anything," I said. "I'll be home around six o'clock. We can grill something for supper. Let me know what you feel like and I can pick it up on the way home."

"Will do," Christian said. "I got things covered here."

I drove to Santa Monica where the new office was located. I'd already hired a skeleton staff who had been working on various startup projects, and now I had to spend a few days finishing hiring the editors and other staff for the California office. It kept me busy for most of the afternoon, my mind focused and forgetting all about everything else.

Around five thirty, I got a text from Christian.

CHRISTIAN: *Hey, how about some nice thick steaks for supper? David said he wants beef.*

JOSH: *I'm on it. Make sure there's some cold beer for me when I get there, and I'll fire up the grill.*

CHRISTIAN: *You got it. See you when you get here.*

. . .

I FINISHED UP AT WORK AND THEN STOPPED BY A WHOLE Foods store on the way home to pick up some beef for supper. When I arrived home, Christian had a cold beer in hand and David was on a lawn chair on the patio in the shade. He seemed pretty good, all things considered.

I went right over to him while Christian got the steaks ready. "How are you doing?" I squeezed his shoulder affectionately.

"Good," he said and gave me a faint smile. "Wish I could have one of those, but I better wait until my antibiotic is finished.

"You should," I said and went over to the grill to start it and get it ready.

We spoke for a while about work and what I was doing with the new office of MBC.

"We had to cancel release of our EP," David said, his voice emotional. "Terry's wife Sharice is having a really hard time, because she just found out she's pregnant."

"Oh, that's too bad," I said and shook my head. David was clearly emotional about it.

"Plus, I just heard about the man and woman in the other car. The man died at the scene, and the woman was airlifted to the hospital with pretty bad internal injuries. She's still in the hospital."

"Do they have any idea why he hit you guys?"

"He spilled his coffee on himself and just for a split second, lost control of the wheel. That was it. One false move and he's dead and Terry's dead. I feel so bad..."

I went over to David and forced him to look in my eyes. "I know you feel bad for them," I said, feeling so bad for him. "There's nothing you can do but look after yourself, okay?"

David nodded, but I could see how emotional he was.

"It should have been me driving, but I had that extra beer," David said. "It should have been me dead. I don't have anyone. No wife, no kids..."

"Don't say that," I replied, frowning. "No one should have died, David. Not Terry. Not the guy in the BMW. It's just bad luck. Not something you can control."

"I could have not had that second beer, but I knew Terry would stop at one. He always had my back when I overindulged."

"It was Terry's choice. I could have driven instead."

"No, then *you* would be dead."

I knelt down beside David and squeezed his shoulder. "David. It was bad luck. Nothing more. It wasn't anyone's fault."

"No, *no*," David said, shaking his head, his eyes brimming. "You're just saying that. If I hadn't had that extra beer, none of this would have happened. We would have left right away and been home without anything happening."

"There's nothing any of us can do about what happened in the past. We have to move on."

"Yeah, Sharice and the new baby and the other kids have to move on. That woman in the BMW has to move on. Tell that to them."

"You're alive," I said and took his hand, squeezing it. "You have to keep living."

He glanced away, clearly not willing or able to accept that fact.

I realized David was suffering from survivor's guilt, and perhaps a delayed response to the crash finally hitting him. He would have some form of PTSD from the crash and from losing his friend and bandmate. It was normal, but it wasn't good. I'd call the nurse at the hospital and see about getting some counseling for David, so he could get over his guilt at surviving while his friend died.

I grilled us steaks and we had a hastily-made salad and some bread for supper, but no matter how hard Christian and I tried, we couldn't pull David out of his funk. Finally, at about eight thirty, David said he was tired and wanted to go to bed, so we helped him to his room and got him ready. I tucked him into his big empty king-sized four poster in his huge room and he looked so tiny against the covers in that huge room.

So alone.

"See you in the morning," I said and kissed his forehead.

"Thanks, bro," David said. "I know I'm not the best company right now."

"Shh," I said and pulled the covers up over his shoulder. "Just go to sleep. You can call me if you need anything in the night. Your cell is right beside you there on the bed."

He nodded and closed his eyes, but I could tell he was still overly emotional.

I completely understood why. He felt responsible for the deaths. He felt guilty for still being alive.

As much as I wanted to go back to Manhattan and see Ella, I wouldn't leave LA until I knew he was getting psychological counseling.

I was now the head of the family, and the brothers were my responsibility.

9
ELLA

Josh texted me at midnight Manhattan time.

JOSH: Hey, pretty lady. How are you? I miss your sweet smile.

I smiled when I read it and texted him right back.

ELLA: I'm fine. I miss you, too. How's David?

I saw the little dots for a long time and realized he was writing a longer text. I hoped it didn't mean David had gotten worse...

Finally, the message popped into my feed.

JOSH: He's fine physically, but emotionally, he's having real problems. He's suffering from survivor's guilt. In addition to Terry dying, the guy in the BMW also died and Terry's wife is pregnant.

ELLA: Oh, I'm so sorry. It wasn't his fault. He wasn't driving, and it was the other guy's fault, right?

JOSH: Yes, it was the other driver at fault. I guess he spilled his coffee and momentarily glanced down and lost control of the wheel. David feels guilty because we stayed, and he and I had an extra beer and so Terry drove instead of him. He figures Terry would be alive if he hadn't.

ELLA: Poor David. You can drive yourself crazy playing 'what if'. Bad things just happen sometimes.

JOSH: I know that, and you know that, but right now, David's blaming himself. I'm going to see about counseling for him. It's hit him really hard.

ELLA: That's good. He needs it, if he feels that way. How are you doing? You were also in the crash and a survivor.

JOSH: I'm fine. Glad to be alive. Sad for the two men who died. I have to be functional for David, so it's taken my mind off myself, I guess. That's a good thing.

ELLA: You have to look after yourself as well. When are you coming back?

JOSH: Once I know that Christian has David's care in hand. He's not teaching this semester so he's happy to stay with David. I'll probably be home in a few days. I'll let you know.

ELLA: Okay.

JOSH: Good night, Ella.

ELLA: Good night. Call me or text me any time you want to talk.

JOSH: I will.

I PUT MY CELL AWAY AND LAID BACK ON MY BED, GLAD that he'd texted me, but worried about him. He felt he had to be strong for his brother, but he was also a survivor and had to take care of himself.

As I tried to fall asleep, I couldn't get the image of Josh in the crumpled SUV out of my mind, aware of how close he had come to being hurt or even killed.

. . .

THE NEXT DAY, I MET MY PARENTS AT THE HOTEL AND WE went out for lunch. Their flight back to New Hampshire left later in the afternoon, so we had time to spare. I took them back to the office while I checked in with Sharon. She'd given me the day off, so I could spend time with my parents before they left, so I left my parents in my office and went to meet with Sharon before we went to the deli down the street.

I had a quick chat with Sharon about Josh, pretending surprise about the accident. I felt bad, but it wasn't time yet to come out and admit we were seeing each other. I wanted to wait until we made some kind of more permanent commitment before I did that.

When I came back, Becca, one of my co-workers was in the office with them.

"Hi, Becca," I said and introduced them.

"Your father was just asking me about you and Keith," she said, her eyebrows raised.

"Yes," my father said, frowning. "She said that Keith already had a girlfriend who works here. Meghan?"

"Yes, as far as I knew, Keith is dating Meghan. I had no idea you two were..." Becca said, shrugging.

"And that Keith is a CPA, not a bicycle courier," my father said, clearing his throat. "It seems that Joshua Macintyre is the one who rides a bike around here. And," he said meaningfully. "There's no bicycle courier business in the building."

"Becca, can you excuse us?" I said, my face hot with embarrassment. "We need to have a chat."

"Okay," she said and had this sheepish expression on her face. "If you want to talk later, we can."

"We should," I said. "Just to clear a few things up."

Becca finally left us and so I closed the door and turned to face my parents, who were looking at me expectantly.

"Tell me you're dating Joshua Macintyre," my mother said.

At the same time, my father said, "Tell me you're not dating Joshua Macintyre..."

They glanced at each other and I could have laughed out loud at how differently the two of them saw the whole business, except I felt sick to my stomach.

"I just made it all up to keep you from worrying about me."

"Keith seemed willing to play along. How come?"

"Because he's a nice guy and realized I had used him as a convenient excuse and went along with it to save me?" I said, hoping it would be enough to throw my father off the trail.

"So, you're not dating Joshua Macintyre?" my father asked, unwilling to give me a break.

"I met him," I said, not wanting to lie, but also not wanting to admit how close we had become. My father opened his mouth to speak but I interrupted him, holding my hand out to stop him. "But we both were burned before and neither of us believe in romance anymore." While that was true, we definitely felt romantic towards each other.

"So, you are dating him," my mother said, smiling.

I stood there, feeling trapped, my fists clenched. "It's not at all what you think. We're friends."

"How do you know what I think?" my father asked.

"You told me that you think he's like his father," I said, reminding him what he'd said earlier about Josh. "You said he was probably a chip off the old block, if I recall correctly."

My father crossed his arms and held my eyes. "When can I meet him?"

Damn...

"You can't and there's no reason to."

"He owns the company you work for. I think that's a good enough reason. Where's his office?"

"He doesn't work here. He's turned over the management of the publishing company to someone else. Besides, he's in California with his brother, who was just in a very bad accident and is recovering." I glanced at my mother, but she was smiling, happy at the thought I was dating a very rich handsome bachelor. "He opened a new office in LA and he won't be back in town for a week or so."

"I'd like to meet him when I'm back in town in two weeks," my father said, placing his hand behind my mother's back. He pointed to the door. "Now that it's settled, let's get some lunch."

My mother gave me this excited smile. She didn't care about Josh's father and his involvement in my father's business partner going to jail. All she cared about was finding me another husband.

Oh, God...

WE HAD A NICE LUNCH DOWN THE STREET AT THE ITALIAN restaurant where Josh and I went for world-famous meatballs. If I could have been honest with them, I could have raved about how romantic it was that Josh took me there when I first arrived, but I didn't want to give out too much info. I hoped to convince my father that we weren't serious, and that he was just a friend. I knew that if he thought were serious, he'd be all over Josh, expecting to meet him and talk to him about life and his views on government intervention in the marketplace or something else he championed as a politician.

Josh was a liberal and my father was a conservative. I figured they'd be like fire and gasoline.

It wouldn't go well, especially if my father brought up his former business partner...

FINALLY, WHEN IT WAS TIME FOR THEM TO GO TO THE airport, we said goodbye and I waved down a taxi to take them to JFK. We kissed and hugged, and my father looked in my eyes, his voice serious.

"I want to meet this Josh when I'm here again."

"Father, it's not what you think. We're not dating."

We're fucking our brains out every night exclusively.

"I know you," he said, shaking his head. "We'll have a drink and get to know each other."

"We're not serious. We're just friends," I insisted, my fingers mentally crossed because I honestly didn't like to lie.

"Just a drink and maybe dinner."

Then he got into the taxi and my mother waved at me through the window as they drove off.

"We're not dating!" I called to the taxi as they drove away.

My mother blew me a kiss.

LATER THAT NIGHT, AFTER I'D FIXED MYSELF A CUP OF ramen and a bagel with peanut butter for supper, I sat down on the sofa and checked my cell for messages. It was still early back in LA and Josh was probably at home with David and his other brother, Christian. I wanted to talk to him, but I didn't want to interrupt, especially if his brother wasn't doing well emotionally.

I missed him. I'd grown used to having him every night since we started to see each other. I hadn't seen him for only three days, but I still felt a hole in my life where he usually fit. I hated the thought we'd be apart for another few days.

Maybe I was falling for Josh, despite my best intentions.

Falling hard.

My cell dinged, and I grabbed it, hoping to see a text from him.

It was my mother.

MOM: *Sweetie, you're going to have to admit to your father that you're dating Josh.*

ELLA: *What makes you so sure I am?*

MOM: *I texted Steph and she fessed up.*

Oh, my God. I was seriously going to kill Steph. She of all people should have known that was in the vault...

I texted Steph right away.

ELLA: *STEPH WHY DID YOU TELL MY MOM ABOUT JOSH???*

The little dots floated away for a good thirty seconds as she replied.

STEPH: *Oh, my God. You didn't tell her?*

ELLA: *No, I didn't tell her! If I had, I would have told you.*

STEPH: *She faked me out. She pretended that she knew you*

were dating Josh and asked me what I thought about it. Seriously, Ella. I figured you told her, and it was common knowledge. I'm so sorry!

ELLA: UGH. Now my father knows, and any chance Josh and I had at privacy is out the window.

STEPH: Seriously, I'm really sorry. She seemed to know and well, you know what your mom is like. She was so excited that I figured you told them when she came down to visit.

ELLA: It's okay. I'll deal with it but damn, I swear that woman could get a confession out of a priest.

I turned back to my conversation with my mother.

ELLA: Mom! You shouldn't have asked Steph. I didn't want Dad to know because he'll pester Josh about his father and the case involving Mr. Harrison...

MOM: Don't worry, dear. I'll work on him. I'm excited that you've met someone already. And Josh is so handsome.

ELLA: He is handsome but he's more than just a pretty face. He's really smart and he's honorable. He's out West looking after his brother. He's the head of his family now and he takes that very seriously. He's a good man, Mom...

MOM: I knew it. You're in love with him. :) :) :) <3 <3 <3

Her text was followed by an annoying string of hearts and smiley faces.

ELLA: I like him, Mom but I'm not in love, okay? Whatever you do, don't let Dad think that we're serious or anything. We're just casual. The last thing Josh needs is for Dad to give him the third-degree.

MOM: *He wouldn't do that. He'd be very interested in meeting Josh and talking to him, but he's got some tact, dear. He's been in politics for years. Give him some credit.*

ELLA: *He has a blind spot when it comes to Mr. Harrison. You know that.*

MOM: *That was twenty years ago. He's mellowed a lot since then. We'll be back in town in two weeks, so if you two are still seeing each other, I want to meet him. Promise me.*

ELLA: **sigh* okay. If we are still seeing each other when you come back, I'll introduce you, but seriously, it's not a big thing. We've both been burned before and neither of us are interested in being burned again.*

MOM: *Then, get married and stay married. Simple. ;)*

I FOUND THE WINKIE EMOTICON THE MOST ANNOYING.

ELLA: EASY FOR YOU TO SAY. FIFTY PERCENT OF ALL *marriages end in divorce. Some engagements don't even make it to the wedding day.*

MOM: *Relax. Let it happen. If it's meant to be, it will be. *Kisses and hugs**

ELLA: *Back at you.*

I PUT MY CELL AWAY AND SAT THERE FOR A LONG MOMENT, wondering how my father would react the next time he was in town. If Josh and I were still seeing each other -- and I hoped we were -- I knew my father would want to meet him.

· · ·

111

ELLA: THE CAT IS OUT OF THE PROVERBIAL BAG.

IN A FEW MOMENTS, JOSH RESPONDED.

JOSH: WHO'S IN THE KNOW? YOUR FATHER?

ELLA: The very one.

JOSH: What happened? I thought you were dead-set against me meeting them. I was willing to, I'll remind you.

ELLA: I pretended I was dating a guy called Keith who was a bicycle courier who worked in the building. Of course, who did we run into but Keith...

JOSH: Ahh. Oh, what a tangled web we weave when first we practice to deceive...

ELLA: Tell me about it. When we were meeting people from the office, my mother mentioned me dating Keith to Becca and of course, she had to correct my mother's mistake. I denied it, but my mother faked out my supposed best friend forever and she confirmed my mother's suspicions. My dad wants to meet you the next time he's in town.

JOSH: Does this mean rapiers at dawn? Do I need to perform six feats of strength and bravery like Heracles?

ELLA: Probably just answer a dozen questions successfully about your father's expose on my dad's business partner, Matt Harrison.

JOSH: I'll read up on the case and prepare. Does your father favor the Socratic method, or will there be a multiple-choice questionnaire?

ELLA: Well, he was in the Military Police before he went to

law school, so I expect the thuMBCcrews and bamboo under the fingernails approach is more likely.

JOSH: I'll make sure to do one hundred sit-ups and pull-ups a day in preparation.

ELLA: I'm so sorry about this. You can bow out if you like and I'll totally understand.

JOSH: Relax. I've been wanting to meet your father since I learned who he was.

ELLA: Really?

JOSH: Oh, yeah. He's notorious. A rainmaker as they call politicians who bring in lots of business to their states. I don't plan on going into politics, but Christian wants to run for public office. Your dad could be a good contact.

ELLA: Okay, but you should be prepared.

JOSH: I'm always prepared. Speaking of which, what are you wearing? *Hint hint*

ELLA: Right now?

JOSH: Yes. Please describe in exquisite detail. Better yet, Skype me. I have a serious need to see you pleasuring yourself.

ELLA: You're in need, are you? *Slowly pulls off her sweatpants and baggy t-shirt to reveal creamy naked skin*

JOSH: That's what I wanted to hear...

AFTER THAT, WE DIDN'T SPEAK ABOUT MY FATHER AGAIN, caught up as we were trying to get the proper angle with our laptops and cellphones, so we could watch each other masturbate to completion.

After my day of stress and frantically trying to deny I was dating Josh, it was a needed distraction.

10
JOSH

Each day saw more progress and by day five of his being released from the hospital, David was sitting up for long stretches of the day, eating far better and being more talkative. He was still preoccupied with being a survivor while his friend and the other driver had died, but he seemed better overall. I had almost wrapped up the work I had planned to finish while in LA at the new office, and so I felt confident that Christian could handle David until the therapist we hired to come in daily and check on him started the following Monday.

I didn't want to leave David, but at the same time, I had meetings and important deadlines back home and needed to leave. Christian was capable, so I knew I could leave and be assured that whatever happened, he could handle it.

"Thanks for coming and spending time with me. And for being there when I needed you."

"Hey," I said and bent down to give David a hug. "Don't mention it. We're brothers. I'm always there for you or any of the brothers if you need me. Seriously. If you want me to come back out at any time, or if you want to come and stay with me out East, you just have to say the word."

David nodded but he looked a bit down in the mouth that I was leaving. We'd been through the event together and I understood how he felt about it, even if I didn't lose anyone close to me.

"Later," he said when I kissed his cheek and gave him a final embrace.

"Call or text me any time," I said, my voice choked at having to leave.

"I will. Give your girl a hug for me. I can't wait to meet her when I come out there."

"I will," I said and waved at Christian. "Come out as soon as you're able."

Then I drove my rental to LAX and waited for my plane.

ONCE OUR PLANE LANDED AT JFK, I STOOD WAITING FOR my limo service and checked my cell to see if Ella had texted me. She hadn't, but that was to be expected. It was the middle of the workday and I had only told her I'd be back in the afternoon.

There was yet another email from Penny, asking for more money, since she'd needed to pay rent.

Sure, Penny. Rent in the middle of the month...

I had to realize that addicts would say and do anything to get their hit. They couldn't help it.

I sent her another hundred dollars and knew that at some point, I'd have to do something to get her on the right track or she'd just kill herself with an overdose.

As I stood reading about the rehab place in California, a man walked by me in the terminal wearing a black fedora. Something about the man made me take notice. Then I remembered the man at Ella's building. I shrugged it off, thinking maybe he was just waiting for someone, but still. I was sure it was the same man.

Once back at the office building in Manhattan, I went up to the apartment to unload my bags and have a quick shower. When I was dressed, I removed a condom from the box I kept in my washroom and slipped it into my jacket pocket, just in case Ella and I were able to find a moment together. I headed down to the MBC offices to check on my inbox and once I went through my emails, the first item on my agenda was to pop into the office of Macintyre Publishing and take a much-needed grope and kiss with my girlfriend.

I sent her a text first, so she could be ready.

JOSH: The photocopier room. 5 Minutes. Be there or be square.

Of course, Ella responded right away.

ELLA: Why, Mr. Macintyre, I do believe that's against the company's fraternization policy.

JOSH: You mean the company's *old* policy that I conveniently ripped up, because I'm the CEO and I can do that kind of thing...

ELLA: You should take care not to take advantage of your power over me to elicit favors...

JOSH: Only if you promise to do the same.

ELLA: What power do I have over you?

JOSH: Just that you occupy my every non-work-related thought almost 24/7 and I salivate with anticipation every time

I think of spending time alone with you. Now, get yourself to the photocopy room toot sweet.

ELLA: Toot sweet? What are you? In seventh grade?

JOSH: Sixth. I'm on my way.

ELLA: Perhaps the photocopy room isn't the best place to meet.

JOSH: I prefer it because it has that forbidden quality to it. We might get caught. It makes everything more intense as a result.

ELLA: Are you into voyeurism perhaps?

JOSH: I'm hoping I'll soon be into your panties.

I TOOK THE ELEVATOR DOWN TO HER FLOOR. I SAID A BRIEF hello to Sarah, the receptionist, and asked where everyone was.

"There's a conference call in the boardroom, but it should be over in about thirty minutes."

"Thanks," I said and found my way through the halls to the photocopy room. With everyone except Sarah in a conference call, I had a brief window of opportunity, which I planned on exploiting to the maximum. When I opened the door, I saw that Ella was already there, a smile on her face.

I closed the door behind me and locked it, then went right over to her, pulling her into my arms.

"Finally," I said, my eyes moving hungrily over her face and body. "Why aren't you in the conference call?"

"It's just for the editors," she said. "Us lowly editorial assistants don't get invited."

"Lucky for me," I replied. "You are a sight for sore eyes."

I kissed her, not giving her a chance to offer a saucy reply.

We kissed deeply, her arms sliding around my neck. She pressed her body against mine, her groin finding mine and feeling my erection. I slid my hands down her back to her buttocks and then slipped a hand under her dress, lifting the hem and running my hand up her thigh to her ... her naked buttock.

She wasn't wearing panties.

"Oh, God," I moaned against the skin of her neck. "What you do to me..."

I slipped my fingers around to her pussy and slid them between her lips to feel her wetness.

"I need to fuck you right now," I said, pulling back, my eyes meeting hers. "Right here on the table."

She didn't hesitate and helped me pull off her dress. She wore a black lace bra and I managed to remove it in no time, burying my face in her magnificent breasts while I unbuckled my belt and unzipped my slacks. I lifted her up onto the table and she spread her legs wide so I could see her beautiful folds.

I knelt between her thighs and covered her pussy with my mouth, licking and sucking her clit and slipping my fingers inside her body. She rested her legs on my shoulders and leaned her head back, her mouth open.

Soon, her breathing became shallower and a flush spread up from her chest to her neck.

"I'm going to come," she murmured. I kept up my tongue's motion on her clit and was rewarded with the sight and sensations of her orgasm, her body clenching around my fingers, her thighs shaking.

When she pushed my head away, I stood and slid the condom I had tucked into my jacket pocket over my erection

119

and then I entered her slick wetness, groaning from the sheer pleasure. We kissed briefly and then I started thrusting inside of her, enjoying the sight of her breasts moving with each thrust.

"Touch yourself," I said, meeting her eyes. "Make yourself come again."

She slid her hand down to her clit and stroked it while I thrust. While she did, I bent forward and took one of her nipples in my mouth, sucking on it before moving to the other.

After a few moments, her eyes became drowsy and she leaned her head back. "I'm going to..."

I thrust harder, knowing that she was close. I wanted to time our orgasms so that we came at the same time, and when I felt her body clenching around me, I was almost there.

"Oh, fuck, fuck..." I groaned as my own orgasm began. I thrust through it, the pleasure blinding.

Finally, when my ejaculations subsided, I leaned over her, kissing her tenderly.

"That was fantastic."

She smiled, her eyes still closed. "It was."

I pulled out and removed the condom, tying it off and wrapping it in some tissue from my jacket pocket. I didn't want to leave it in the garbage can, so I tucked it back into my jacket pocket.

"We don't want to leave evidence of our indiscretion lying around."

She smiled and pulled on her bra, then after I finished zipping and buckling up, I helped her on with her dress. She smoothed her hair and then ran her fingers through mine.

"That's better. No one would have the slightest inkling that you'd just got laid in the photocopy room."

"Good. I have a reputation to maintain," I said with a chuckle. "Now, I better go, or someone will try to get into the room and we'll be discovered."

We kissed briefly, and I unlocked the door and checked the hallways. Luckily, they were empty and so I left the floor, saying goodbye to Sarah on my way to the elevator.

"Is everything okay, Mr. Macintyre?" she asked, tilting her head to the side.

"Everything is amazing," I replied with a smile. I pressed the elevator button and waited for it to arrive, whistling a tune while I waited.

When I arrived at my own floor, I went right to my office and closed the door behind me.

It was sure good to be back home.

I SPENT THE REST OF THE DAY CATCHING UP ON BUSINESS that had piled up while I was away. I should have stayed late and worked until nine to make up for it, but I planned on taking Ella out for a nice dinner somewhere, so we could spend some quality time together. While our encounter in the photocopy room was very sexually satisfying, I needed more. I wanted to hear about her parent's visit and how she managed while I was away. For the past month since we started seeing each other, I'd grown used to falling asleep with her in my arms and talking to her every evening and I missed it.

JOSH: I NEED A GOOD STEAK AND BAKED POTATO FOR supper. I think they also make the most delicious crème brûlée.

Care to come join me? There's a great steak and chop house on Lexington.

Ella responded soon after.

ELLA: You had me at good steak. What time?

JOSH: How about six thirty? Come up to the apartment and we can go from there.

ELLA: Okay. See you then.

I CALLED THE CEDARS SECOND CHANCES REHAB FACILITY to talk with the intake coordinator about the best way to approach Penny. We spoke about how an addict had to be ready for help and I said I would call back when I had more of an idea whether Penny actually wanted to get sober.

She had to. How could she be happy living that way?

I pushed Penny to the back of my mind and at just after six o'clock, I cleaned off my desktop and left my office, taking the elevator up to the apartment. Once there, I freshened up a bit, brushing my teeth and hair. Once I was ready, I stood at the kitchen island and checked my cell for news from David.

There was a message from him waiting for me.

DAVID: Hey, bro. What's up? How are you doing being back in the Big Apple?

I sent him a response right away.

JOSH: Glad to be back but miss you. Hope Christian's looking after you. Let me know if you need anything.

DAVID: We're good. Send me a pic of you with your new woman. I can't wait to meet her.

JOSH: Will do. I know she'd love to meet you, too.

DAVID: Thanks for coming out to LA and being there when I needed you.

JOSH: I was glad to be with you. Make sure you get some counseling for the PTSD.

DAVID: I'm fine. Seriously. I know I'm lucky to be alive. I just hope we can pull together and keep the band going. It's going to be a while before we can find another drummer like Terry.

JOSH: Take it slow. You need to look after yourself first. Your fans will still be there when you're ready to go back onstage.

DAVID: Hope so.

JOSH: Take care. Love you.

DAVID: Love you back, bro.

I closed the thread and sat back, rubbing my eyes, wondering if David was as good as he was making out to be. At least Christian was with him. I didn't want David to be alone. After a personal loss like that, after a trauma which he felt responsible for causing, David was vulnerable. I wished he was living in Manhattan instead of LA, so we could all be together. But LA was David's home and where his band mates lived.

I could hop on a plane at any time if needed to go out there and spend time with him, so I tried to put it out of my mind.

The door to the apartment opened and in walked Ella, looking beautiful as usual. She was wearing the same black dress, prim but still form fitting, showing off her delicious curves. She had a coy smile on her face and came right over to me where I stood at the kitchen island and slipped her arms around my neck.

"I missed you while you were gone," she said and pressed her lips against mine.

"We fucked only two hours ago in the photocopy room," I

said with a laugh. "But I could tell how much you missed me by how fast you came today."

"You were pretty fast yourself," she said and leaned back, giving me side eyes. "I take it your sessions with Mr. Manuel didn't quite satisfy your needs."

"I have many needs," I said and kissed her again. "You are one of them and I can't ever seem to get enough. But right now, I need a thick juicy steak and a glass of beer and a nice warm bath and then more of you in my bed."

"I'll take it."

We kissed once more and then left the apartment for the restaurant.

WE GOT A SEAT NEAR THE WINDOW AND SAT HOLDING hands across the table. The restaurant was busy, but not too busy so I got my favorite table. I hadn't taken Ella there yet and so she was in for a treat. I knew she loved beef, so she'd be in heaven for the chef bought only grass-fed and pastured beef and aged it extra-long. It was a carnivore's paradise.

We ordered and while we waited for our food to come, I saw a man walking by who seemed familiar. I then remembered seeing him earlier in the day at the airport and outside Ella's apartment building, for he was wearing the fedora with a feather in the brim. Now, I knew for certain that it was too much of a coincidence that I saw him before and then outside the restaurant.

He walked by our window and I saw him glance inside. Our eyes met briefly but he kept walking and didn't show that he recognized me, but I recognized him.

What the *hell?* Manhattan was a huge city. There was no way he was there coincidentally.

"Excuse me for a moment," I said and stood, leaving Ella and slipping out the front door. I checked the direction he'd been walking but couldn't see him because of the thick pedestrian traffic.

I went down the street about a block, looking for him but he'd disappeared completely. He may have gone into one of the stores but if so, I didn't see him when I walked by, checking inside through the windows.

Foiled in my attempt to find him, I went back inside the restaurant and sat back down across from Ella.

"What happened?" she asked and squeezed my hand when I took hers.

I saw someone," I said. "Someone I saw outside your apartment last week and then again today at the airport. It was just too big of a coincidence to see him outside this restaurant tonight. He glanced inside and saw me. I felt like he recognized me and then looked away a bit too quickly. Almost guiltily."

"That's strange," she said. "You saw him outside my apartment? You're sure it's the same man?"

"Same black hat and raincoat." I shrugged, trying not to make too big of a deal of it. "I'll talk to Mark in Security and see if he has any ideas."

For the rest of the evening, I put the man out of my mind and focused on Ella. We discussed the accident and Terry's death, how David was doing and how he wanted to meet her.

"Let me take a picture of us together," I said and held out my cell. We leaned in together and I tried to get a good perspective.

"Can I help you with that?" the waitress asked on her way by.

"Yes, thanks," I said and handed her my cell. Ella and I leaned in together, still holding hands, and we smiled for the camera. The waitress snapped a couple of pics and then handed the phone back to me. We checked the pics out and I sent one to David, with a message that read, *Here we are, enjoying a nice steak at Mandy's in Mid-Town.*

I knew he'd be happy to see us together.

About half an hour later, I saw the same man walk by again. This time, I ran out, not even saying anything to Ella. I almost tripped over the stairs on my way out, but once again, by the time I got out on the sidewalk, he was nowhere in sight.

I stood in the middle of the block, watching, but he didn't appear out of any storefront.

Whoever he was, I was sure he was following me...

I went back inside and sat back down.

"Did you see the man again?" Ella asked, her brow furrowed.

"I did," I said. "But I lost him again."

"Maybe he knew your father and wanted to say something but didn't want to interrupt your dinner. If he's an old friend or something, he'll come by."

"Could be."

It was just too much for me to think it was accidental. Whatever the case, I was unnerved by it. I'd never hired a bodyguard before, but I was considering it now. The very last thing I wanted was some nutcase to target me -- or Ella. My father's television empire and news channel had been a target before of disgruntled viewers who didn't approve of our political leanings. Ella's own father had a grudge against my father because of past news coverage of his former business partner.

I'd speak with Mark at the security company that worked for MBC and see what they suggested.

WE WALKED BACK TO THE BUILDING, AND I HOPED ELLA would agree to stay with me in the apartment for the night. Although we'd already had great sex in the photocopy room, I wanted her in my bed.

My king-sized bed, rather than her Murphy bed in her apartment in Chelsea.

"Are you staying with me tonight?" I asked when we reached the door.

"I thought you'd never ask," she said and smiled up at me. "I even brought a change of clothes and have them hidden away in a drawer in my office just in case I needed them."

"I've slept alone enough this past two weeks," I said and pulled her against me. "I want to fall asleep with you and wake up with you."

We kissed and then went inside the building. I nodded to the security guard at the front desk and seeing him made me think once more about the man I'd seen who I suspected was following me. I decided to talk to Mark, the security guard at the front desk and check into hiring someone to watch my back for a few days, see if they could see anything worth noting. Many of the guards had been in the service and had training in reconnaissance. They'd make good bodyguards in case I ever needed any.

I walked Ella to the elevator and kissed her quickly. "You

go up. I'm going to talk to Mark about the man I saw following me."

"Do you really think he was following you?"

I nodded. "I have this sense he was trying not to be observed, but he failed. I'll be up in ten."

"Okay," Ella said and pressed the button. "You're scaring me."

"I don't mean to, but it raised the hair on the back of my neck when I saw him for the third time."

She nodded, and the elevator doors closed.

I went out to the security desk and leaned on the counter.

"Hey, Mark. Do any of you guys have any training in protection? I'm thinking of hiring a bodyguard because I think I have someone following me."

"Oh, yeah, sure," Mark said. He removed the hat he wore and rubbed his forehead. "You should talk to Reg. He has a couple of guys who did some bouncer work before and were involved in military police over in Iraq and Afghanistan. You think someone was following you? Tonight?"

"Yeah," I said and hesitated, feeling a bit crazy for even mentioning it. "I saw the same guy at the airport and then twice when I was out tonight. When I tried to follow him, he disappeared."

"What did he look like?"

I shrugged. "Fifties, stout. Had this old fedora on with a feather in the brim."

"No shit," he said and frowned. "That sounds like someone I saw hanging around outside the building earlier tonight. Guy my age, long raincoat, black hat. Could be a stalker."

That made me feel extra nervous, but I resisted. "Could also be someone completely innocent. Let me know if anyone at the head office is interested in doing some protection work for me for a couple of weeks. I'll make it worth their while on short notice."

"Will do. In the meantime, I'll keep my eyes peeled and will let the next shift know about it, so they can keep a watch out. You should call Reg. He'll be able to help."

"Much appreciated," I said and left the lobby. I took the elevator up to the penthouse, glad that I had at least started the process of hiring someone to act as a bodyguard until we had a better idea who it was who was following me and why...

11

ELLA

I woke up in the middle of the night to find Josh sitting bolt upright in bed.

"What's wrong?" I asked, my heart racing.

"Oh, damn," he said ad ran a hand through his hair. "I'm sorry I woke you. I had a nightmare."

He lay back down and rolled over to pull me into his arms.

"What was it about?"

"The accident," he said, his voice sounding exhausted. "I was trying to pull David out and the SUV was on fire."

"I'm so sorry." I stroked his shoulder. "I think it's normal after something traumatic like that to have nightmares."

He shrugged. "I saw worse that than over in Afghanistan," he said softly. "Dead bodies, blown up from IEDs, firefights, outright murders. I should be able to handle the accident better."

"This was your brother," I said and kissed him. "It's harder to take when it's a family member. You have to give it time. Once David's back completely healed, it will get better."

"I hope so," he said and exhaled, burying his face in my neck. "I think the man following me just set off my alarm bells."

That worried me too, but I didn't want to make too much of it. Josh had enough on his plate as it was.

"Don't worry. Soon, you'll have a guard in place and you won't have to worry."

It took a while, but eventually, we both fell back to sleep.

WHEN I WOKE, JOSH WAS ALREADY UP AND HAD BEATEN me to the bathroom to brush his teeth. It was a regular battle between us to see who could get there first.

"Beat you," he said, his toothbrush in his mouth, his amused eyes meeting mine in the bathroom mirror.

"No fair," I said and hip-checked him out of the way so I could get my own toothbrush ready. Soon, we were both brushing and smiling at each other like a couple of teenagers, and once we were both finished rinsing, he pulled me into his arms and kissed me.

"We have time before work," he said and wagged his eyebrows suggestively.

"Shower or bath?" I asked, pulling away.

"Shower," he said.

We got dirty before we got clean.

AFTER I FINISHED DRESSING AND FIXING MY MAKEUP, I went to the kitchen where Josh was talking on his cell. He turned and saw me and held his finger up for a second.

"Okay, I'll come right down. I'll be interested to see it."

He ended his call and placed his cell down on the island countertop carefully.

"What's up? Who were you speaking with?" I asked, when he came over and pulled me into his arms.

"Now, I don't want to freak you out, but the security manager, said they caught some video of a man about fifty-ish with a fedora that has a feather in the brim hanging around the building. I'm going down to check it out, but I suspect it's the same man I saw at the airport. If so, I want you to be extra careful and not go out alone. I'm going to hire a bodyguard to ghost both of us."

"Why me?" I asked, frowning, a chill running through me. "I'm no one."

"You're crazy, right? Your father is Governor Carlson of New Hampshire..."

"If anyone is the target of a nutcase, it would be you. You have all the money."

Josh nodded and stroked my cheek. "Whatever the case, I want you to be careful. No going anywhere alone, okay? At least until we learn who this yahoo is."

"Okay..." I said doubtfully. "I think it's unnecessary on my part."

"I'm serious. Promise me."

I sighed. "I promise."

"Good. I don't want to have to worry that someone's planning to abduct you for ransom or anything."

We kissed again and then I went down to my office. I sat down behind my desk and opened my laptop, then read emails for the first fifteen minutes, but my mind kept going back to what Josh said about me being a potential target of a kidnapper because of my father's position as a Governor. My father had security in Concord, of course, but I never had any worries. I tried to brush it off, but a sense of unease descended over me that nothing seemed to dissipate.

At around ten thirty, Josh popped into my office and closed the door behind him.

"Josh," I said, surprised that he had come to my office. "What are you doing here?"

"I saw the security video from last night."

"And?" I asked, my heart beating faster.

He took in a deep breath. "It's definitely the same man."

"Oh, Josh," I said in alarm. "What do you think he was doing?"

He shrugged. "Hanging around the building, watching for me, or you -- or us. For a while he stood across the street from the front entry and pretended to read a newspaper, but he kept a pretty close eye on people entering or leaving the building. Then, he crossed the street and stood outside, also pretending to read his paper. He stuck around for about half an hour and trailed us when we walked down the street to the restaurant."

"That's so creepy," I replied. "Who do you think he is?"

Josh folded his arms. "I have no clue. He could be a disgruntled employee who was fired. He could be a former business associate of my father's who is here to find out what happened to my father. He could be a private detective collecting info on me or you. He could be a nutcase, planning on harming one of us for notoriety or for some grudge."

"What do you think?"

He shrugged. "I have no idea. The best option would be a friend of my father who is curious about me but didn't want to bother me in public. We were out having dinner and maybe he didn't want to intrude. But if that was the case, he could have come up to my office at any time and introduced himself. The next best would be a private detective doing some research on me for a client. Could be my ex trying to find some dirt on me. Who knows?"

"And the worst?" I asked, although I already knew. I held up my hand. "I know. A crackpot who had a grudge and was trying to find a time to hurt you. Or me."

"I'm afraid so. Whoever he is, I want you to be extra careful until we know for sure. I'm meeting with the head of the firm that provides security for the building and will arrange to hire someone to act as a bodyguard. I should have done this a long time ago, but my father never had one and so I didn't think I needed one either. But there are nutcases out there who have weird political ideologies and think journalists and news organizations are fair game. We should be prepared just in case."

"Okay," I said and swallowed hard. "Now, I'm really nervous."

"I don't want to alarm you, but we should err on the side of caution in this case."

He came over to where I sat and bent down, kissing me quickly.

Just then, Sharon popped her head inside the door. When she saw Josh bending over me, she gasped a bit.

Josh stood up straight and stepped away.

"Hi, Sharon," he said and turned to me. "I'll talk to you later."

He passed Sharon, who stood in the doorway, at a total loss for words.

When Josh was gone, Sharon turned and watched him go down the hallway. Finally, she came inside and closed the door to my office.

"It's none of my business, but are you two a thing?"

"Yes," I said, deciding not to try to lie, given she probably saw him kissing me. "Please don't say anything about it to the other staff. Neither of us wants it to be a public issue."

"I understand," she said. "You can count on me to zip my lip."

"Thanks," I said. "Neither Josh nor I want any fuss made. Both of us have been burned before by office romances and so we're really hesitant."

"Mum's the word," Sharon said. "Can you come to my office for a chat? I have some questions on a few manuscripts and I was passing by your office from a meeting, I thought I'd ask you instead of sending a text."

"Sure. Do you want me now?"

"Might as well. Bring your notebook."

I grabbed my black Moleskine notebook and followed her down the hall, glad she was willing to keep mum about Josh and my relationship. I hoped she wouldn't see it as a negative thing and turn against me. She didn't seem to, but in the shock of seeing us together, she may have just been nice about it.

I'd know in the next few days or weeks if it would be a bad thing between us. If I was seen as the boss's girlfriend, she might feel uncomfortable.

I ARRIVED BACK AT MY OFFICE AFTER OUR MEETING WAS finished and spent the rest of the morning working on my pile of manuscripts that I had to get through before the end of the week. I checked my cell and didn't see anything from Josh, so I worked through my lunch, grabbing an apple and yogurt I had stowed in the office refrigerator, so I didn't have to go out and get anything.

About three o'clock in the afternoon, I was ready for a break and checked my cell once more. Still nothing from Josh, so I took a break and slipped on a pair of running shoes I kept in my office, put on my sunglasses, and left the building, needed a cup of decent coffee. Then, I wanted to go for a walk and get some air. I'd been cooped up all morning and part of the afternoon and needed a change of scene.

It was then I remembered that Josh wanted me to take extra care and not go anywhere without his bodyguard.

I stood in the lobby and texted Josh.

ELLA: I'm in the lobby and want to go for a walk, get some exercise. Where's this bodyguard you want to follow me?

Josh wrote back right away.

JOSH: Hold on. I'll come right down.

I waited by the tall picture windows overlooking the street, wondering how long we'd have to keep up the bodyguard thing, hoping it wasn't too long. I liked my personal freedom and the ability to pick up and go wherever I wanted whenever I wanted.

Still, who knew who that strange fellow was with the hat and feather? If Josh was nervous and he'd been over in Afghanistan, who was I to question the need for a bodyguard?

A few minutes later, Josh appeared out of one of the elevators and came over to me.

"Hey," he said and gave me a quick kiss. "Come with me. I'll introduce you to Reg. He's going to be ghosting us for a few days."

I followed Josh to a room at the back of the building near the rear exit. The sign on the door read, Building Security, and

Josh knocked and glanced up at the small security camera in the corner above the door.

The door buzzed open and we went inside. A guard wearing a security uniform that read SecureForce sat behind a desk. In front of him was a bank of monitors, showing various views of the building's interior and exterior and the back alley.

"Wow," I said, watching pedestrians and office workers coming and going. Cars drove up in the back alley and workers unloaded boxes at a service bay. "I didn't realize the building had this kind of security system."

"Oh, yes," Josh said. "Gotta keep things secure."

We went past the security guard and into another room where a man dressed in a business suit sat behind a desk. He stood when Josh entered, and the two men shook hands.

"Reg, this is Ella, my girlfriend. Ella, this is retired Sergeant Reg Collins, who's going to be providing us with security when we leave the premises."

Reg and I shook hands and the man was huge, strong, and reminded me of someone you'd see on a professional wrestling show with his shaved head and beefy body.

"Nice to meet you, miss," he said in a gravelly voice. "I hear your father is Governor Carlson from New Hampshire."

"He is," I said and smiled. "Do you know him?"

"I haven't had the pleasure."

I nodded and turned to Josh. "What do I do?"

"You send Reg a message and he'll meet you at the front door. He'll follow behind you a few feet and keep an eye out for anything suspicious."

"What if I want to go on the subway?"

"Take the limo service if you need to go anywhere," Josh

said. "I've told them to expect a call from you now and then when you need a car."

"Are you sure?" I said and frowned. "Is this really necessary?"

"Miss, until we know who this man is who followed you and Mr. Macintyre, it's best to be careful. It's no problem for me or the car service. It's our bread and butter."

Reg smiled at me, his eyes twinkling like he was amused.

"Okay, if you really think it's necessary."

I turned to Josh. "I just want some air and to get a coffee. I thought I'd walk around the park for fifteen minutes or so."

"I'd join you, but I have a meeting in five."

I turned to Reg. "If you don't mind?" I said.

"Lead the way," he replied and nodded to Josh.

We left the security office and Josh gave my arm a quick squeeze before he left to take the elevator back up to his office. On my part, I left the building, slipping on my sunglasses and taking the sidewalk.

I spend the next twenty minutes walking along the external walkway along the east side of Central Park. Then I stopped in at my favorite coffee shop and got a latte, so I could finish off the day.

Reg stood a few feet away from me, his hands crossed in front of him.

"Can I get you anything?" I asked him and pointed to the counter at an array of pastries and drinks.

He shook his head. "No, thanks Miss. I'm fine."

I paid and returned to the Macintyre building, Reg a few dozen feet behind me. Once I got inside, I stopped, and Reg came over to me.

"I'll wait until you get on the elevator."

"Okay, if you think that's necessary," I said.

"I do," he replied and folding his hands once more.

I went to the elevator and pressed the button, then waited, coffee in hand. Finally, the elevator opened. Reg nodded to me and then I entered, seeing it was empty.

Finally, the elevator doors closed, and I went up to my floor, feeling a bit strange that there was so much fuss made about my whereabouts.

I hoped they found out who the man was soon.

LATER THAT AFTERNOON, STEPH CALLED ME, AND I WAS so excited to see her name, I actually gasped.

"Steph, I haven't heard from you in weeks," I said, smiling as I imagined her sitting in her dorm in her sweats and hoodie, her Mickey Mouse slippers on her feet. Although we texted each other a lot, we hadn't actually spoke in person.

"I know, girlfriend, I decided to give you a call. I have Monday off and thought I might come down to Manhattan. I talked to my prof and I can skip class on Friday so that'll mean we can spend the whole weekend together. I mean, when you and Mr. Big aren't going at it."

I laughed. "If you're here, we won't be going at it, believe me. I need to spend my time with you. Mr. Big can spend time in his office catching up with work or something."

"Okay, but I don't want to interfere too much with your budding romance. If you need to spend time with him, I'll understand and can take a trip to a day spa and luxuriate or something."

"Not on your life. While you're here, I'm all yours."

"Okay, girlfriend, I'll see you on Friday night. Pick me up at Penn Station?"

"I'll see you there. Oh, I'll be with a bodyguard, so be prepared."

"Oh, you guys actually have one? I can't believe it. I guess a guy as rich as Josh would need one."

"Luckily, a guy as rich as Josh can afford one. They're damn expensive. You don't just have one guy. You have five. Three for each day and two spares in case on or two of them are sick or killed."

"Oh, God, don't say that."

"Don't worry," I said and tried to downplay it as much as possible. "It's just a precaution."

"Okay. See you soon, kiddo. Smooches."

"Smooches back."

I hung up and smiled, looking around the office.

I had to get my work done so I could enjoy my weekend with Steph.

12

JOSH

The week went fast as I tried to get caught back up with my workload and Reg's security team watched for a return visit from the mystery man with the feathered fedora.

He didn't show for a couple of days, but one day, I got a call from Reg, and a request that I come down to the security office. He didn't give me any details, but I suspected it was because Mr. Fedora, as Ella and I had taken to calling him, had returned.

I left my office and made my way down to the lobby, wondering what was up.

I buzzed in at the security office and glanced up at the camera, then went inside once the door opened.

Reg was standing with his back to the door, looking over the shoulder of the duty guard watching the security monitors.

"Hello, Sir," Reg said. Sorry to interrupt your morning but I thought you should see this."

"Good morning, Reg. What have we got?"

Reg pointed at one of the monitors, which showed the area

directly in front of the building. The camera zoomed to show across the street, and there, standing in an alcove in partial shadow, was Mr. Fedora.

"I thought you might want me to go over and question him," Reg said in a low voice. "I could ask for ID."

"If you think that's appropriate," I said. "See what he says."

"Sounds good," Reg said and pulled out his sunglasses. "I'll be right back."

Reg left us, and so I sat beside the duty guard and watched on the video cameras. It showed Reg leaving the back of the building and walking through the lobby to the front door. The next camera picked him up as he stood at the side of the road and checked for traffic. Then, it followed him as he jaywalked directly across, threading his way through the cars, which were lined up waiting for the lights.

Mr. Fedora was reading a newspaper -- or pretending to -- and when he saw Reg come across the street directly towards him, he appeared to try to disappear behind the paper, and stepped farther back into the alcove. Reg went right up to the man and he disappeared behind Reg's bulk. We watched for a few moments, and then Reg returned, crossing the street the same way he had before, dodging traffic expertly. Mr. Fedora left the alcove, tucked the paper under his arm, and walked away, disappearing from the security camera's view.

Reg finally returned to the security office and the duty guard buzzed him inside.

"Well?" I asked when he came over to where we sat. "What's the upshot?"

"The man refused to identify himself or state his business, so I told him if he didn't leave, I'd call the police and they'd find out who he was and why he was there."

"Okay," I said and shrugged. "I guess that's all we can do, right? The man has every right to stand outside the building if he wants."

"The police can't do anything unless he issues some threat or physically accosts you," Reg replied. "But they could ask for his identification and we could find out who he is that way."

I nodded in understanding. "Keep an eye out for him. If he returns, call the police."

"Will do."

I went back up to my office and sat behind my desk, unhappy that we hadn't been able to answer the question of just who this man was and why he was hanging around outside the building. There was no law against what he was doing, so we couldn't have him arrested. Until he did or said something, all we could do was watch and wait. He now knew that we were aware of him, so that was something.

I didn't think the man was a threat -- at least, he didn't seem like someone who was personally threatening but you never knew.

LATER THAT DAY, I TEXTED ELLA, DECIDING TO INVITE HER for dinner out since both of us had been eating at our desks in order to catch up with work and working late. Ella had elected to stay at her own place for a couple of days since her friend from Concord was coming down to Manhattan for a visit.

JOSH: Hey, are you up for some Thai food? I know a great restaurant in the area. I have to work late, but it would give us a chance to catch up. I haven't seen you for two days and I'm dying here...

ELLA: Sure. I'm dying, too. I was surprised you didn't ask for an emergency photocopy room meeting...

JOSH: That was hot, but I'm hoping you'll stay with me tonight so we can store up a few orgasms while your friend is in town.

ELLA: Mr. Macintyre. You make it sound like currency in a bank account. I don't know if I should be flattered or upset...

JOSH: It's like currency and worth its weight in gold. I need a deposit in my bank account or I'll go into overdraft.

ELLA: !!!

ELLA: I'll stay tonight but Steph is coming into town tomorrow, so I won't be making any deposits while she's here. I hope you understand.

JOSH: I'll suffer. Mr. Manuel and I will become reacquainted.

ELLA: At least you'll be able to visit with Mr. Manuel. I, on the other hand, will not be able to have a visit from B.O.B., since my bestie will be sleeping on the bed beside me...

JOSH: Hmm. Two beautiful ladies sleeping in the same bed. You have to know where a man's mind goes...

ELLA: !!! Not that there's anything wrong with that, but we don't play for the other team, even when there's a drought.

JOSH: I could rent you a nice suite at the Ritz and then you'd each have your own room for her visit. In fact, consider it done.

I quickly opened a window in my browser and searched for the Ritz-Carlton Central Park. I reserved a suite with two bedrooms. Luckily, my credit card was already entered in since I had an account with them.

ELLA: Josh, I couldn't accept that.

I smiled.

JOSH: *If you don't, the place will go to waste, and my money will be spent for nothing because... I already reserved it. It's paid for and the matter is finished. I don't want to hear another word about it. You've been working extra hard the past two weeks, and this is just a bonus in recognition.*

ELLA: *Josh...*

JOSH: *Ella...*

ELLA: *I still won't be meeting with B.O.B., though. I'm going to save up all my lust for when Steph goes back to New Hampshire. Then, I plan on overindulging in you.*

JOSH: *That's what I like to hear. I'd say that I'd do the same, but it's a plumbing issue.*

ELLA: *You can't go three nights without a visit from Mr. Manuel?*

JOSH: *I could, but then my mind would get backed up like a sink or toilet and you wouldn't want that.*

ELLA: *So, the plumbing affects the command and control center?*

JOSH: *They are intricately linked. Screw with one and the other is toast.*

ELLA: *We could sext after Steph goes to bed. She's a deep sleeper.*

JOSH: *Sounds like a plan. I'll pick you up at 6:30. We can walk there. It's just a few blocks away.*

ELLA: *See you then.*

FOR THE REST OF THE AFTERNOON, I TRIED TO WRAP UP AS much of my work as possible, so I could spend time with Ella over dinner and enjoy our last night together before the weekend and Steph's visit.

I was interested in meeting the famed Stephanie, Ella's best friend from high school. Apparently, she encouraged Ella to see me despite everything and so I owed a lot of my recent happiness to her. While I would miss Ella in my bed for the weekend, I wouldn't dream of keeping the two women apart.

At just after six, I left the office and zipped up to the apartment to change into something a bit less formal, then I went down to Ella's floor and popped into Sharon's office on the way. She was still working hard, her head in her laptop.

"Hey," I said. "How are you doing? Everything going as planned?"

"Absolutely," she said and glanced up. "You here to pick up Ella?"

"Yes," I said and stepped inside. "I hope you're okay with it. Neither of us really think office romances are wise, given our histories, but life intervenes."

"That it does. Of course, I'm fine with it. Josh, your personal life is your personal life and so is Ella's. As long as it doesn't interfere with her productivity, I'm all for letting people leave their work at the office."

"Good," I said. "I don't want you to worry that you can't treat Ella the way you'd treat any intern. That's why I hired you and promoted you -- because I know you'll always be fair, and you have high expectations. My relationship with Ella doesn't change anything in my view and expectation."

"Message received." She gave me a quick salute and smile.

I smiled back and went down the hallway to Ella's office. I knocked on the door and slipped inside.

"Are you ready?" I asked, coming over and leaning down to give her a quick kiss.

"Always," she replied with a coy smile.

"Oh, what you do to me." We kissed again and finally, she shut off her computer and grabbed her bag.

"Let's go."

WE STOPPED AT THE SECURITY OFFICE AND REG followed us out of the building and down the street. When we went inside, he remained outside the entrance, his hands folded, watching the pedestrians to see if there was anyone following us. I felt bad that it had come to hiring a bodyguard, but until we knew who the mystery man with the fedora was, I would rather be safe than sorry.

The Thai restaurant was cramped with patrons, enjoying the delicious aromatic food.

Our table was in a corner out of the way and gave us some privacy. We ordered Pad Thai and other delicacies and leaned into our food, both of us eating as if we hadn't eaten for hours.

Which I hadn't. I realized I only grabbed an apple for lunch, so this was the first food I'd eaten since noon.

"This is sooo good," Ella said, slurping down the noodles. "I love the lime."

"It is good," I replied. "I was over in Thailand for a vacation and really got into it. Now, it's a staple."

We spent the next hour trying various dishes and when we were finally full, I leaned back.

"What do you say about a ride around Central Park?"

"Oh, that sounds nice," Ella said with a smile.

"I promised I'd take you some night. If not now, when?"

"My thought exactly."

After I spoke with Reg about the carriage ride, he agreed to trail us on the trip in a second carriage. Then, we walked out into the evening as the sun was beginning to set. When we got to 7th Avenue and 57th Street, just outside Central Park, I hired two of the carriages for a tour. I paid for the longer tour, and we climbed in, pulled a blanket around us and sat beside each other and enjoyed the ride, with Reg trailing us a few dozen feet behind.

I slipped my arm around Ella's shoulder and pulled her closer. Together, we took in the beautiful scenery as the last of the leaves had turned and fallen. It was still beautiful, but the colors had already peaked but at least we could enjoy the crisp autumn air.

Of course, it also reminded me of my almost-wedding a year earlier. We even had plans to marry in the park and have our pictures taken on the bridge. All that planning came crashing down and although I was happy now, there was still a part of me that hurt from the betrayal.

I pulled Ella closer and kissed the top of her head, then kissed her lips. She was not at all like my ex, conniving and calculating. She was open and honest and more interested in doing something of value rather than being rich.

She was the kind of woman I could see myself spending the rest of my life with.

In fact, she *was* the woman I could see myself spending the rest of my life with.

It surprised me that I thought that, so soon after meeting her, but I did. I never grew bored with her company and there was always something to talk about. We both loved books, writing and reading. While my focus was on journalism and hers was fiction, we shared a love of the written word and could talk for hours about the latest book we read.

When the ride was finished, the three of us walked back to

the building and the apartment, hand in hand, enjoying the sounds and sights of night in Mid-Town Manhattan.

"I always dreamed of being here," Ella said to me, swinging our arms as we walked up to the building.

"Really?" I said, still surprised at the mystique that Manhattan held for so many people who lived outside its borders. "I always dreamed of living somewhere with real scenery. Like Colorado or even Seattle. Mountains. The ocean. All I see around me here is concrete. Which reminds me, we still haven't gone to the house in Montauk. You have to come and see it. That's where I'd really love to live if I had the chance."

"You could," she said. "Why not?"

"I need to be close to the office because of the *The Chronicle*. Maybe someday, but not for the next few years."

"I'd love to see it, though. Some weekend when you feel you can get away, we should take a drive there."

I lifted her hand to my lips and kissed her knuckles. "It's a deal."

I could see us spending weekends there in the summer and pictured her in a bikini lying on the beach that bordered our property. My property, actually.

It was the gift my father bequeathed to me, and it spoke to how well he knew me. How well he knew each of us.

"Let's go upstairs. I have to ravish you thoroughly before tomorrow when I have to give you up for three whole nights of time spent with Mr. Manuel."

She smiled and pulled me into the elevator. By the look in her eyes, I knew we'd more than make up for it.

13
ELLA

Reg said goodnight and went to the security office while we entered the elevator and made our way upstairs. We'd kissed the entire trip in the elevator, lucky that the building was pretty empty.

"Isn't there a security camera in here?" I asked, glancing up at the corners.

"Somewhere," Josh replied. "Who cares? Give them a thrill."

I pulled Josh into the apartment, and as soon as we got inside and closed the door, I kissed him, my hands reaching down to unbuckle his belt.

"Mmm," he murmured against the skin of my neck. "Impatient, are you? I like it."

"I'm always impatient for you," I said and pulled down his zipper, reaching in to feel his hardness.

"I'm always ready for you," he said, his voice throaty with desire.

He groaned when I took him in my hand and squeezed,

153

enjoying the hardness. I fell to my knees there just inside the door and took him into my mouth, wanting to drive him a bit crazy before we even got to the bedroom.

"Oh, God, Ella," he said and leaned against the door, his slacks and boxer briefs on the floor around his shoes. "You are such a tease."

I sucked him in and cupped his balls in one hand while I gripped his shaft with the other. When I pulled off with a wet pop, I glanced up and met his gaze. "I always come through, though, don't I? Not all tease..."

"No, you tease me in the best way possible."

I smiled and then took him back into my mouth, my lips pulling off and pushing onto the head of his cock, my tongue lapping around the rim.

Finally, he groaned and pulled me up. "You have to stop, or I'll be finished before we even start."

"You like?" I asked, giving him a coy look.

"I like very much," he said. "Too much. Come."

He shucked off his shoes and pants, then pulled me into the bedroom and began stripping off my clothes while I removed his, until we were both naked.

"You are so fucking lush," he said as he sat on the bed and pulled me closer to him. "I want to eat and lick every inch of you."

"Every inch is yours," I said, my body vibrating with desire.

He pressed his face into my breast, taking the nipple between his lips and sucking. The sensations went from my nipple right to my clit and I moaned, my eyes closed. He moved between my breasts, sucking each nipple, squeezing them together so he could lick from one to the other.

Then he stood and turned me around, pushing me back onto the bed and spreading my thighs with his knees.

He leaned over me and kissed me, taking my hands into his and holding them above my head.

"You're mine," he said, his voice gruff.

"I am," I replied, a catch in my breath at the sound of possession in his tone. I was his -- all his. Every part of me.

Then his mouth claimed mine in a blistering kiss and all conscious thought fled, replaced by pure pleasure.

WHEN WE WERE BOTH SPENT, WE LAY ON OUR BACKS staring at the ceiling, catching our breath.

"That was so good," I said and glanced at him.

"It was," he said and reached over to stroke my cheek. "You can expect more of that in the morning. Maybe at lunch, too, if I can weasel out of my one o'clock meeting. If I'm going to miss three nights of you, I expect to make it up in the next twelve hours before Steph comes."

"I won't complain," I said and smiled.

"Somehow, I knew you wouldn't," Josh said with a laugh.

JOSH KEPT TO HIS PROMISE OF MAKING ME WEAK-KNEED with lust twice more before the next afternoon. We met in the apartment during lunch and had sex standing up in the living room, with me leaning over the sofa and him behind me, both of us half-dressed. This was after an early morning bout in the shower as we prepared for the day.

As Josh pulled out of me and removed his condom, I closed my eyes and remained standing as I was, thighs spread.

"I'm going to need an afternoon nap," I said with a smile. "Do you think the boss will mind?"

"I think the boss will have to call in and cancel his one o'clock meeting," Josh replied and did just that. "You should ask for the afternoon off and we could spend it on the sofa or in bed."

"I can't," I said and stood up finally, pulling up my thong and pulling down my skirt. "I promised I'd get some work done for Sharon before the weekend, so I could take Monday off and spend it with Steph. But given you have an in with the big boss, you definitely should take the afternoon off and lie around like a sloth."

I turned around and watched as Josh fixed his own clothes. "Nope. Boss is a damn slave driver so I better not. Besides, I wouldn't enjoy it without you." When he was finished buckling his belt, he came over and pulled me into his arms. "I'll go back like a dutiful CEO and do my meetings."

We kissed.

"Text me later when Steph is in bed if you want to talk. Or anything."

"Or anything," I said with a grin. "Like I can't guess what that means..."

He smiled back. Then he reached into his jacket pocket and pulled out a black Ritz-Carlton keycard.

"This is for you and Steph. Indulge your every womanish whim. The spa. A meal in the restaurant. Room service. Whatever you feel like."

"You are far too sweet," I said and took the keycard, shaking my head. "I can't believe you did that."

"Believe it, use it, and enjoy it. Thinking of you two having fun will be what keeps me from being sad without you."

We kissed, and then kissed again and again. Finally, I pulled out of his arms and left the apartment, taking the elevator down to my office. I planned on eating my lunch alone in my office, so I could leave early and meet Steph at Penn Station. While I was happy as a lark to see Steph, her visit was unexpected, and it seemed to break the momentum of Josh and my relationship, which had reignited when he returned from California, feeling even more substantial since then. We were inseparable and didn't want to be apart. While I had finally felt right about seeing Josh after my initial reluctance, now I was certain that he was who I wanted. Everything about him was perfect. I couldn't think of a single thing that I didn't like and while I knew it was probably still a large dose of infatuation, I liked to think it was also just a serious compatibility between us.

We fit together so well in all things.

I LEFT WORK EARLY AND TOOK THE CAR SERVICE TO PENN Station, my stomach all butterflies at seeing Steph again. I waited by her gate and checked to see if the train was on time. Luckily, it was and soon, there she was, the same old Steph I'd known since we were both in our Freshman year of high school in Concord. Two of the nerdiest nerds in our schools.

Steph was tall and lanky, and often said she reminded herself of a giraffe but to me, who was on the shorter side of female height, she was like a thoroughbred with her mane of long blonde hair and blue eyes. The only thing that kept her from being a model was her love of all things scientific, otherwise, she could have been on the catwalks of New York and Milan. She'd even done some modeling when she was a girl for local stores in Concord but when her mother pushed her to consider becoming a model, she'd rebelled.

She hated being looked at. She felt ridiculously tall and lanky and had knock-knees and was pigeon toed. Otherwise, she was very attractive in a Daryl Hannah sort of way.

"There you are," she said and hugged me, almost picking me up in her glee. She pulled back. "You look great. I see Mr. Big has been good for you. You've got that rosy-cheeked hue you lost when Jerkface betrayed you."

I patted my cheeks dramatically. "You like my hue?" referencing a favorite Seinfeld episode.

"It's a lovely hue."

We walked arm in arm to the limo that waited on the curb outside the station and Reg drove us to Central Park.

"Why are we here?" she asked when we arrived across from the Ritz-Carlton. "Don't you live in Chelsea?"

"We're in for a real treat," I said and held up the Ritz-Carlton keycard Josh had given me before I left.

"What's that?" Steph asked, her mouth open. "Is that what I think it is? Is that a Ritz-Carlton room key?"

"The very thing." I handed it to her and she took it like it was something delicate and breakable.

"Oh, my God," Steph said and stroked it in mock-worship. She sniffed it and then rubbed it on her face. "It's the real deal. The Ritz."

"It is. We have a suite, with two bedrooms. Josh wants us to use the Spa and eat dinner in the restaurant and order in room service. The works."

"Seriously? I thought he'd resent me for coming down and horning in on you."

"Not at all. He said it would make him happy to think of us living it up."

"He is too sweet," Steph said. "I feel kinda bad, but I'll take it. I'll take it willingly."

We went inside and checked in, excited to have the suite to ourselves for three glorious days. We took the elevator up and walked down the hallway to our rooms, and both of us gasped when we saw the interior. I was familiar with the layout because of my previous stay with Josh, but Steph was totally impressed and turned in a huge circle, covering her mouth with her hands.

"Oh, my God, Ella -- it's amazing. I can't believe we have this to ourselves. What do we do first?"

"Whatever you want. We could just kick back and have a drink, watch a movie and gab. Whatever."

"That sounds perfect. How about we get a snack from room service, have a couple of drinks and you can fill me in on all the juicy details about Josh. I can't wait to meet him."

"He wants to meet you, too. He'll meet us for lunch or a drink tomorrow or Sunday, if you want."

"I want, I want. Maybe he has a brother who needs a wife? I'm on the market."

We both laughed and then set about to picking our rooms and getting our clothes and makeup and personal items out of our suitcases, so it felt more like home. When we were done, we went to the main living room, which was richly appointed in golds and dark brocade and flopped on the plush sofas. I ordered up some trays of appetizers from room service and we had drinks from the small bar fridge. Steph had a vodka cooler and I had a glass of white wine.

"To a girl's weekend," Steph said. "For two old friends lucky to have the chance to get together in such a posh place."

"To us," I said and clinked my glass against her bottle.

We talked for a while about Josh of course, for he was the most important event in my life since I left Concord and got my internship.

"I missed our girl talks with you gone and texting just doesn't cut it," Steph said. "So, is Josh better than Jerkface in the boyfriend department?"

"Much better. Like night and day. I never realized it, but Josh is just so much more laid back than Jerkface ever was. Jerkface was always so aware of how everything looked and what people could do or not do for him. I thought it was just ambition, but it was more -- it was a kind of narcissism. Josh is so different. He's really focused on his work, but he really wants to make The Chronicle a success. He's committed to journalism as an important part of American democracy and he wants to make sure the paper lives up to its former reputation."

"And he's good in bed?" she asked, her eyes twinkling.

"Steph!" I said with a laugh.

"You knew I'd ask. Come on -- fess up. He must be good in bed or you wouldn't stick around. Right?"

"He's more than good in bed," I admitted, smiling as I remembered our last session just hours earlier in the apartment. "He's fantastic in bed and out of it. In the shower, on the sofa, on the floor, on the desk in his office..."

"Ohh, you're getting in some hot office sex, are you?"

I grinned. "Yes. And it is hot. I never thought I'd enjoy risky sex, but I do. Even though I can lock my office door and he can his, there's always the chance that people will realize we're in the office doing it."

"So that box is ticked. He's good in bed. What else? Why do you like him? Sell him to me."

I made a face as I considered Steph's question. What did I like about him?

"He's fun. He has a great sense of humor. He's really nice. He's got some values and morals. He joined the Army, he went to college and studied journalism. He's just a really great guy."

"And so good looking. I mean, he's hot, Ella. You are so lucky."

"He is," I said and smiled to myself, thinking of him with his longish hair that flopped in this incredibly sexy way in his eyes at times. His very blue eyes. His well-trimmed beard covering a very square jaw.

Our room service food was delivered and for the rest of the night, we gabbed and ate and watched a movie, catching up with each other's business.

It was good to have her visit and it was so sweet of Josh to rent us the hotel suite, so we could do it in comfort and style.

By midnight, we were both tired and so we hugged and went our separate ways, Steph to her room and me to mine. I got into my nightgown and brushed my teeth, washed my face and wondered what I'd find when I opened up my cell. I had promised myself I wouldn't check it once while Steph and I spent the evening together and I kept to that promise. So, I was excited to see what Josh would write when I did check. Would he want to Skype and watch me? Or would we just talk?

Honestly, I was tired at that point, but I knew if he tried, he could get me worked up enough for some sexting.

I checked my messages and there was one from Josh, send over an hour earlier.

JOSH: I have to make a quick trip out of town. Something came up out of the blue and I'll be gone all weekend, but I should be back on Monday. Sorry about this. I really wanted to meet Steph tomorrow, but we'll have to reschedule. Tell her I'm sure you two can find something to do to pass the time with me gone.

I frowned, wondering what came up that would require him to go out of town. Was it David? Had something happened to him and Josh needed to go to look after him?

ELLA: Is everything all right? Is it David?

Josh didn't reply, and I wondered if that was the reason -- had he flown back to California and was unable to respond.

I was saddened that I didn't get a chance to text with him before I went to bed, but I was tired.

ELLA: I'm going to bed, but I'll text you first thing in the morning. I hope everything is okay. Let me know. XOXOXO

I put my cell away and cursed myself that I didn't check sooner.

I lay awake for a while, my mind going to all the possible issues that might take him out of town. Was it the paper? Was it David?

I hoped that when I woke up, I'd have an answer.

14
JOSH

The phone call came early in the morning.

It was from the police department in Millbrook. I knew right away what that meant -- it was Penny and she was probably in jail and needed me to bail her out.

"Hello, Penny," I said, unable to keep the disapproval out of my voice. "I take it you're in jail and want me to pay for your bail."

"I'm sorry," she said, her voice breaking with emotion. "Yes, I was arrested with some dope on me and they took me in."

"I'll make arrangements," I said, exhaling heavily. "But only if you agree that you need help."

"I need help," she said, sobbing. "I need help, okay?"

"Will you go into rehab if I pay for it?"

There was a pause. I knew it was of no use to go into rehab if you weren't ready and willing to accept help, but perhaps Penny was there, now."

"Yes," she said finally, her voice soft. "I will. I'm sick of this. Anything has to be better than this."

"Okay," I said. "I'll fly there, bail you out and I'll get you a place at this rehab facility in California. All the big stars use it and their program has been really successful."

"Thank you," she said, and I heard her sniffing. "Why are you doing this?"

I paused, having to think about why. It wasn't that I felt anything for her. I never had, but I could do something to help her. I could help her get sober and maybe start over. For Grant.

"Because I can. I'll see you later today."

As I dialed the rehab facility, I thought about why I was really doing it.

There was a residual bit of guilt I felt about being so cavalier about her back when we were fucking. I had never taken her seriously, for I made it clear to her that I wasn't in the market for a girlfriend and she had said she felt completely the same. She was focused on her future, getting a degree and a job, not marriage or children.

At the time, I felt no guilt about having casual sex with her whenever I came to Montgomery with Grant on leave. We kept the relationship, such as it was, secret, because she didn't want Grant to know. I thought it was no big deal. We used each other so it was mutual.

I had no idea she was hoping it would turn into more because she never once gave me the idea that she wanted anything more.

When I met Christie the following year and fell in love, I stopped going to Montgomery as often and when I did, I made it clear I was now seeing someone seriously and couldn't sleep with her.

I thought that was that. End of story.

Obviously, Penny didn't feel the same way. I didn't know if

her downward slide started at that point or if she was struggling with addiction when we were together, but whatever the case, she'd fallen far since I had last seen her.

Luckily, the facility had a bed and could take Penny in that night, if I showed up with her. I made arrangements to fly from Montgomery to California and rented a car, so I could drive her to the facility.

My money was good for something.

I packed a small overnight bag and sent Ella a text to let her know I'd be taking a trip out of state and wouldn't be back until Tuesday.

I'd stay with David for a few days while I was in California and then I'd fly home, taking the red-eye flight on Monday. I would arrive back home on Tuesday morning.

Then Reg drove me to JFK to catch my flight, having just enough time to get there. I'd chartered a private jet to take me to Millbrook and then to California because of scheduling. It was just easier and the timing was better that way.

WHEN I ARRIVED IN MILLBROOK ABOUT FOUR IN THE afternoon, Penny was much more sober and in a very bad mood. Of course, she was hurting, and sick from withdrawal. She looked a total mess, her hair greasy, and her clothes wrinkled from having slept in cells. I paid her bail and she signed out of the jail and came out to the rental car with me.

"Now what?" she said sourly. "You gonna save me from myself?"

"You have to save yourself, Penny. I'm just offering you a place to go."

She nodded, and I hoped she understood. "I'm sick. I need

something to take off the edge or I'll be throwing up on the plane."

She had to fly to California, so I had to get her manageable. I didn't approve of her doing her drugs, but she couldn't fly in the condition she was in and I had no intention of driving all the way to California.

I called the facility and spoke about her with Steve, the manager of the facility in California.

"She won't be able to go on the flight the way she is now. She's been in the jail overnight. Should I let her shoot up first?"

"Do what you have to do to get her here," he replied. "We'll take care of her once she arrives and make sure she's able to get clean."

I relented and gave her money so she could buy some of her drugs. We stopped at her place and she shot up and then packed a bag, showering briefly and changing her clothes before we drove back to Montgomery to catch the jet to LAX.

SHE WAS QUIET ON THE FLIGHT AND SLEPT MOST OF THE way there, a blanket around her and the window screen down so it was dark. I spent the time reading financial reports and wondering what happened to her that made her start doing harder drugs. Once we touched down and disembarked, I picked up the rental and drove to the facility located in the hills outside LA.

We arrived at nine thirty and I carried her bag up the steps to the entrance. The place was dark, but I could see it was nice, with clean modern furnishings that had a boutique hotel feel to the place.

"This is nice," Penny said as we walked to the front door.

"Better than I thought."

I held the door open and we went inside. We were met at the security desk by a middle-aged man with a balding head and a pair of half-eye glasses perched at the end of his nose.

"Penelope McNeil, I presume?" he said and waved us into his office. "Mr. Macintyre? I'm Frank Tillerson. We spoke on the phone earlier. Come in."

For the next half hour, we did intake for Penny and she signed papers. I'd already paid for the six-week program, so all we had to do was get Penny to sign the waivers and agreement to follow the rules.

"Well, that's it," Frank said. "I'll take her back to her room and get her settled for the night. That's all I need from you."

I went to Penny, who looked so small and afraid, her eyes wide.

"Good luck," I said and squeezed her arm. "Let me know how things are going."

She nodded but said nothing, so I left the room, left the facility, and got in the car.

I sat for a moment and read my cell, wondering if Ella had texted me, but she hadn't.

I was never so glad to be leaving a place as I was that facility, hoping that the experts could help Penny get clean.

I DROVE BACK TO BRENTWOOD AND ARRIVED AT THE mansion close to midnight. David was still up, waiting for me.

"Hey, bro," he said, standing at the front doors. "Welcome back. Busy saving people's lives, are you?"

I shook my head. "All I did was pay for the program. She has to save her own life."

"Well, you're my hero, even so."

I went inside, and we had a quick chat about Penny and what happened between us several years earlier.

"Most guys would have just written her off," David said, shaking his head.

"She was my best friend's sister. I fucked her maybe a dozen times over the course of two years. I feel responsible for her in some way. Or at least, I feel like I could help."

"Like I say, you're my hero," David said opened his arms for a big hug. "Now, I have to hit the hay, get my beauty sleep if I hope to finish this damn EP. I have a new musician coming in to take Terry's place this week and we have a lot to go over if I hope to finish it on time."

We hugged for a long moment, and then I went to my room and to bed.

ONCE I WAS UNDRESSED AND LYING IN THE HUGE KING-sized bed, I sent Ella a text, feeling bad that I hadn't told her about the whole mess with Penny. I still felt bad for my role in her eventual personal crash, whatever that might be.

JOSH: Just to let you know I made it to LA and will be back on Tuesday. I'll be staying with David for the rest of the weekend but I'll call you so I can hear your voice.

Ella got back to me right away, like she was waiting for my text. When I checked, it was the middle of the night her time.

ELLA: Josh, I hope everything is okay with David.

JOSH: Sorry to wake you up in the middle of the night. David's fine. I had something personal to follow up on related to Grant's death. We'll talk about it when I get back. It's not something I'm proud of.

168

ELLA: You can tell me anything. I won't judge. Seriously, Josh. I want to be there for you if you need moral support or whatever it is. You were there for me when my life crashed around me.

JOSH: Thanks. We'll talk about it when I get back. It's still pretty raw.

ELLA: Okay. I miss you. XOXOX

JOSH: Miss you too. XOXOX

I imagined her in the hotel room at the Ritz lying in the bed, wearing her pretty black nightgown and worrying about me and what I'd left town about so mysteriously. I'd sit down with her when I got back and explain everything.

Of course, I tossed and turned for an hour, my mind going over everything that happened between Penny and me and my complete and total ignorance of how she truly felt. Had I been so callous as to not recognize that she thought there was more between us?

I WOKE UP IN THE MIDDLE OF THE NIGHT WITH ANOTHER nightmare, my body covered in sweat, my heart racing.

This time, it was Grant I was trying to rescue, pulling him out of his car, which had slammed into the base of the bridge, the engine erupting into flames. I couldn't save him, beat back by the fire, but I kept shouting his name, trying to pry the door open, bracing my foot against the side of the car and pulling with all my might.

"Grant! Grant! Grant!"

I sat up in bed, panting, struggling for a moment to remember where I was. Soon, my pulse slowed, and I realized it was just another nightmare. It was four o'clock in the morning. That was the fifth nightmare I'd had in the past two weeks.

I needed to get some counseling.

IN THE MORNING, I HAD A QUICK SHOWER AND JOINED David on the patio to watch the sunrise. It was glorious, and I stood beside him and breathed in the air.

"Pretty sweet, isn't it? You sure you don't want to leave the Big Apple and come out here for the weather?"

"You might be able to talk me into it one day, but not yet."

We spend the day together, and as much as I needed to get back to Manhattan, I wanted to take the time and spend it with David since I was already out there and Ella would be with Steph. David seemed to be doing much better than when I last saw him, although he was still pretty weak from the surgery.

"How are you?" I asked as we lounged beside the pool later that morning. "How's your recovery going?"

"Good," he said, but his voice didn't sound so good. He sounded exhausted. "Well, as good as can be expected." He gave me a smile, but it appeared forced, like he was playing for the cameras and wasn't doing quite as well as he made out.

"So, you've got a new musician coming in to help finish the EP?"

"Yeah, but I don't know if he's going to work out. He doesn't know any of the new songs and it's going to take a lot of work to get him up to snuff."

"It takes time to do anything well, I guess," I said, trying to be supportive.

David shrugged. "Maybe this album's just a write-off. Maybe I have to accept that it's just not going to happen."

"Give it time," I said and reached over to squeeze his arm.

He exhaled but didn't respond. He wasn't doing quite as well as he made out.

"I'm worried about you," I said. "You have to give yourself time to get over the accident. You need to heal, and you need to deal with your survivor's guilt. You know that, right?"

He glanced over at me. "You, too, with the survivor's guilt? That's what Jake said. How can I get over something that's true? I can't deny Terry died because of me."

"David, Terry died because the other guy spilled his coffee and hit your vehicle. Not because of anything you did."

"It's because I wasn't driving. I *should* have been driving," he said, making a fist and hitting it against the chair's arm. "I shouldn't have had that extra beer."

"Well, then I'm responsible, too. I shouldn't have agreed to have another beer, either. If I had said no, you wouldn't have had that beer and we would have left earlier and none of this would have happened. In fact, if I hadn't come out for a visit, if I had stayed at a hotel, it wouldn't have happened. You'll drive yourself crazy if you try to assign blame to yourself for what happened."

David shook his head, seemingly unable to understand or accept that it wasn't his fault. "I can't escape responsibility even if I want to. It should have been me. He had kids, man..."

Of course, that made me think of Grant and his two boys and a sense of darkness descended over me.

All I could think of was sleeping in, lying on the beach, and not worrying about anything -- not Penny, not David, and not mysterious Mr. Fedora.

I needed a break from all the drama.

I wanted Ella beside me.

15

ELLA

After Josh texted me in the middle of the night I laid back in bed and tried to go back to sleep, but I couldn't help but wonder what personal thing had come up that he had to deal with relating to Grant's death. What could he possibly have done that he wouldn't be proud of relating to Grant?

Was it Grant's widow or kids? My mind did all kinds of mental gymnastics trying to figure out what he would not be proud of relating to Grant's death. Part of me wished Josh hadn't told me anything because now I was obsessed.

I tossed and turned quite a bit before sleep took me once more.

In the morning, I woke early and had a shower, needing the hot water to feel better. I was tired after waking up in the middle of the night and struggling to fall back to sleep.

When I came out of the office, Steph was in the main bathroom having her own shower. We met in the kitchen and looked over the room service menu.

"Josh said he wanted us to indulge ourselves, so we can order anything we want."

Steph's eyes widened. "In that case, I want the works. Eggs Benedict. Waffles. Fruit. Coffee. Juice," Steph said.

"You got it." I called up room service and we sat down in the living room and waited for our food to come.

"What's up with your man?"

"I don't know," I said and frowned remembering our strange discussion in the middle of the night. "He said he had a personal matter to deal with that he wasn't proud of. It had something to do with his friend, who committed suicide and whose funeral he attended. It means he had to fly to California. He's going to stay with his brother and will be back on Monday, so unfortunately, he's not going to be able to meet you."

"That's too bad," Steph said. "I wonder what he could mean by the not proud part."

"I have no idea. Your guess is as good as mine. Do you suppose it has to do with the man's wife? Maybe his parents? I just can't think of what Josh could have done that he wouldn't be proud of. He's a really good man."

Steph shrugged. "He'll probably tell you when he gets back."

"I hope so. He's been having nightmares lately and I wonder if he isn't under a lot of stress and is feeling survivor's guilt."

"His friend did die. He's probably feeling bad that he hadn't kept in touch with him or something. When he gets back, he'll tell you."

"Why wouldn't he tell me now?"

"Give him time," Steph said. "His emotions are probably too raw. You know what men are like."

"I know," I said. I wanted to be patient, but I felt bad that Josh didn't feel able to tell me right away. Why?

Our food came and the two of us indulged, stuffing ourselves with the delicious food. Then, after I called Reg and arranged for him to come and ghost me for the day, Steph and I spent the morning walking through Central Park with Reg in tow. We stopped for a while by the lake and took in some sun, for it was a warm autumn day.

"I feel weird having Mr. Sunglasses following us. I wonder who Mr. Fedora is."

"Me, too. Hopefully, it's just a private detective doing some business research or something innocuous. What do you want to do?" I asked. "Anything special?"

"Just the usual tourist traps," Steph said. "I want to take the subway. I want to go down Fifth Avenue and I want to go to Ground Zero. Plus, maybe the Museum of Modern Art."

"That sounds like a perfect day," I said, happy to be going out and spending the day with Steph, doing touristy things. I'd been so busy with work and with Josh, that I hadn't done a lot of just wandering.

OUR DAY WAS ENJOYABLE AND BY THE TIME WE GOT BACK to the hotel at six that evening, we were both exhausted.

"What do we do for supper? Feel like going to the restaurant?"

"I'd love it," Steph said.

So, we got dressed up and went down to the restaurant

lounge for a drink before a lovely meal of beef burgundy and dessert comprised of a special maple cheesecake.

"I don't know about you, but I want to get into my jammies and watch a movie. What do you say we watch whatever blockbuster is on the pay-per-view?"

"It's a plan.

So we did.

By midnight, I was exhausted and hoped that Josh would text me soon, so I could go to sleep.

JOSH: *How was your day of fun with Steph?*

I smiled when I saw his text and replied.

ELLA: *It was perfect. We ordered room service for breakfast, Reg ghosted us all afternoon while we did touristy things, and then we had a lovely diner at the restaurant. We watched a movie and now, we're both in bed, ready to sleep.*

JOSH: *In bed??? Both of you??? Enquiring minds...*

ELLA: *In our separate beds.*

JOSH: *A man can dream. :) Seriously, I'm glad you had a good day. That's why I wanted to get the hotel suite for you while Steph is there.*

ELLA: *How about you? How was your day?*

JOSH: *It went by. I'm spending the night with David. We had a nice day by the pool and a barbecue for supper.*

ELLA: *What about the personal issue? Did you take care of that? Are you going to tell me about it?*

JOSH: *I will. It's not something I'm proud of. When I get back, we'll sit down, and I'll tell you. I'm just glad I had to chance to make things right -- or at least try to.*

ELLA: *You know you can tell me.*

JOSH: *I know. I will, in person.*

ELLA: *Okay. You have me worried about what it might be.*

JOSH: It's a sensitive issue. I want to do it justice and I can't via text. I hope you feel you can trust me.

ELLA: I do. When you're ready to tell me, I'm ready to hear it.

JOSH: I appreciate your patience. I needed to take care of a thing and so I did. I was in the area and decided to stop in and check on David. He's not doing as well as I would like.

ELLA: Oh, I'm so sorry. Is he having trouble getting over his surgery?

JOSH: No, he has survivor's guilt. He feels responsible for Terry's death. I've tried to convince him that he's mistaken, but he's pretty down about it. I think he needs therapy and am trying to encourage him to get some help. I may have convinced him.

ELLA: It must be so stressful for you. You're a survivor of that accident as well. How are you doing?

JOSH: I'm fine. I'm managing.

ELLA: Any more nightmares.

JOSH: Yes, but that's probably because of Grant. I'll be fine.

ELLA: You need to look after yourself as well. You're the big brother but you may need therapy as well.

JOSH: When I get home, I want you and I to take a trip out to the house in Montauk. I want to spend the entire weekend just lying around on the sofa in front of the television. And enjoying each other.

ELLA: That sounds wonderful.

JOSH: Great. I'll make it happen as soon as I get back.

ELLA: I can't wait.

JOSH: I'll let you go to bed now. I miss you.

ELLA: I miss you, too.

I put my cell down and lay back on the bed, glad that Josh

wanted to go to Montauk for a weekend. I missed him, and as much as I was glad to have Steph in town, I wished I was in bed with Josh instead of being alone.

THE NEXT DAY WAS A BLUR OF PERSONAL INDULGENCE IN the hotel spa, in the restaurant, and during our touristy trip around Manhattan, always followed or accompanied by Reg, my trusty bodyguard. Josh would be coming home early in the morning on Tuesday, so he'd miss meeting Steph, but we agreed to meet up one weekend when we went to Concord -- maybe for Thanksgiving. Josh would meet Steph then.

Reg drove Steph and I to Penn Station on Monday after lunch to catch her train back to New Hampshire leaving at two o'clock. We hugged each other before she had to leave to catch her train.

"I'm so glad you didn't let me buy you a ticket back to Concord that day you called me," Steph said, tears in her eyes. "You've got it good here. I can't wait to move here, too, and hopefully, Josh can introduce me to one of his hunky friends."

"That would be awesome," I said and squeezed her tightly. "Make sure to Skype me whenever you feel like it."

"I will."

She left me and went to her track, waving at me as she went down the stairs. Then she was gone, and I was alone. I sighed heavily, happy to have had Steph for the weekend, and sad to see her go, knowing I probably wouldn't see her again until Christmas, which was almost a whole month away.

I turned and saw Reg standing by the stairs, his hands folded as he waited patiently for me.

"Well, Reg. I guess it's time to go home."

"Lead the way," he said and pointed to the escalator that went to the upper platform. He followed me up and out of the station to the vehicle and opened the door for me when I arrived. I sat inside in the back and watched the streets of the city pass by on the way back to my apartment in Chelsea.

ONCE THERE, I PACED THE SPACE, FEELING A BIT LOST now that I was alone. Josh was still in California with David and Steph was on her way home to Concord. I was alone. I stood at the window and looked down at the courtyard behind the apartment building. It was late afternoon by then and I wondered what secret thing Josh had to tell me that he felt so embarrassed about. While I stood there, I saw a man enter the alley behind the apartment building and felt a shock go through me when I noticed he was wearing a fedora.

I picked up my cell and took a quick picture of the man and then called Reg.

"Hey, there's a man in the back alley wearing a fedora. Should I be worried?"

"I'll check it out. Stay in your apartment."

I ended the call and watched from the window, standing behind a sheer curtain, hoping that it hid me from his view. He was standing smoking beside a door to another apartment building across the alley and for all I knew, he was just a resident there and wasn't Mr. Fedora, but I wanted to be sure.

Soon, I saw Reg crossing the alley and approaching the man. They spoke and finally, the man threw down his cigarette and left the alley. Reg watched him and then returned to the apartment building. I'd given him a spare key, so he could come in and meet me when I needed him, so he came right up to my apartment and knocked at the door.

I opened it after looking through the peephole.

"It wasn't the same man," Reg said. "He's a resident of the building and can't smoke in his apartment because of his wife's emphysema."

"I'm so sorry," I said and shrugged. "I couldn't tell if he was the same man from my apartment. It's far enough away that I couldn't make out his face."

"No problem," Reg said. "Better safe than sorry. If you ever have any fear about a situation, if anything raises your alarm bells, call me and I'll come right away."

I frowned. "Do you think I'm a target? I thought you two figured the man was after Josh."

"Can't be sure until we know who he is. Both you and Josh could be targets, although given his wealth, Josh is more likely the one someone would be interested in."

I nodded and felt a little better. At least the man knew Josh was aware of him and that Josh had a body guard to watch over him -- over us.

"You can go home now," I said. "I'm going to stay inside tonight. I'll call you when I'm ready to go to work tomorrow morning, but it'll be the usual time."

"See you then. Good night."

"Good night," I replied and closed the door behind him, locking and double locking the door.

Reg went back to his vehicle.

I WENT TO BED EARLY THAT NIGHT AND BEFORE I WENT TO sleep, I texted Josh, wanting to connect with him in some way.

ELLA: Hey, there. How was your day? Steph is gone and I'm all alone back in my tiny studio apartment on my Murphy bed. I expect you're on your way to the airport to catch your red-eye flight. Can't wait to see you when you get back.

I didn't hear back from him right away, so I pulled my covers over my shoulder and closed my eyes, hoping that life would return back to normal the next day, but there was a tiny bit of unease inside of me as I tried to go to sleep.

Who was the man with the Fedora following Josh and me? What had Josh done that he wasn't proud of relating to Grant?

16
JOSH

I spent the the next three days in LA with David, trying to feel him out and decide whether I should stay longer or whether he was good enough, so I could leave him. Luckily, a couple of his band members came by later in the afternoon on Monday and they convinced him to go into the studio and practice their new songs for the EP. I saw him brighten up considerably and thought that as long as he was busy working on the new release, and had people around him, he'd be okay.

I had dinner alone by the pool, leftover food from the night before, while the band played, totally absorbed in whatever song they were working on. Finally, around eight, about half an hour before I was scheduled to leave, David emerged from the studio, his expression satisfied.

"That was a good day's work for a change," he said and plopped down on the lawn chair beside me. Up above us, the sky was clear, and the stars were beginning to peep out in the growing dark. "Sorry if you were all by yourself."

"I'm a big boy," I said and smiled. "I caught up on some reading and got my dose of Vitamin D to last me for the rest of the year."

"Oh, yeah. You have to go back to Manhattan and winter. I don't know how you can live there. I need sun and surf to be happy."

"I think I'll take Ella out to the house in Montauk, speaking of surf. The weather isn't all that nice at this time of year, but we can walk the beach, and enjoy the house."

"Sounds like a good escape for you. You've been working extra hard the past few months."

"Year," I said, thinking about how focused I had been since Christie and I split. I had a one-track mind after we broke up and it had kept my mind off my heartbreak. "It's going to pay off. The paper is starting to take shape. I think by the new year, it should be ready for re-launch."

"Cool," David said. "I'll make a trip to Manhattan for the event."

"That would make me happy. When do you think your EP will be released?"

David shrugged. "If things keep going well, maybe before Easter. That would be optimal, so we'll get a lot of sales and then maybe, I can do a tour in the spring once we see how sales go."

"I'm sure sales will be fine," I said, surprised that there was even any question. "People are already calling it the band's 'much anticipated new release'."

"Yeah, but every new release is still a gamble. We've done some different things this time, and now with a new member, well, the feel will be different from what our fans are used to. I just hope people are happy."

"I'm sure they will be."

I stood. "Well, I have to pack up and get the car ready for the drive to the airport."

"Sorry I missed supper with you, but when you're in the groove, you have to stay there until it's over."

"I totally understand," I said.

David followed me into the house and to my room on the second floor. I finished packing my overnight bag and then I grabbed my jacket and slipped on my shoes.

"I'm as ready as I'll ever be. Good to see you again, brother," I said, and we hugged. I kissed him, and we patted each other on the back before breaking the embrace.

"Anytime, bro. You bring that pretty little woman out with you the next time you come, okay? I'm dying to meet her."

"I'll try," I said. "Maybe you can come out east for Christmas."

"I'll see where we're at with the EP and let you know, but I'll do my best to make it, no matter what."

"Good," I said and got into the rental car. "Take care."

"You, too."

Then I drove off, watching him standing in the driveway in my rear-view mirror. I felt a little better leaving him, knowing that he was happier with the way the recording of their EP was going. Hopefully, he'd get better and better, and the success of the new record would make Terry's loss easier to bear. I imagined all the brothers sitting around a big table at the house in Montauk for Christmas and decided to make it happen.

I arrived at the airport and turned in the rental car, then checked in for my flight back to JFK. I boarded and sat in my first-class seat, then after getting settled in, I checked my messages.

ELLA: Hey, there. How was your day? Steph is gone and I'm all alone back in my tiny studio apartment on my Murphy bed. I expect you're on your way to the airport to catch your red-eye flight. Can't wait to see you when you get back.

I smiled and sent her a reply that I knew she wouldn't get until she woke.

JOSH: I had a good day. David and the band practiced and recorded all afternoon, so it was me alone by the pool. I'm on the plane and will be home soon. See you tomorrow in the photocopy room at some point for a squeeze and kiss, and more if I can manage it.

Then, I closed my cell and leaned back, planning to catch some shuteye after the plane taxied down the runway for takeoff and we were finally in the air.

I ARRIVED BACK AT JFK AT ELEVEN O'CLOCK THE NEXT morning and was met by Reg, who drove us back to the apartment.

He told me about the small bit of intrigue when Ella saw a man wearing a fedora in the back alley behind her apartment in Chelsea and I thanked him for being there to calm her fears.

"No sign of Mr. Fedora since the day you spoke with him?"

Reg shook his head. "No sign. We'll keep an eye out for anyone or anything suspicious."

"Thanks," I said. I went up to the apartment and had a quick shower and then made my way to my office to try to get a few hours of work in before I popped in to see Ella. I'd been away for three days and while I was on top of my email, there were papers to sign and reports to read. Plus, editorial meetings I had to attend and prepare for.

Just before two o'clock in the afternoon, I sent a text to Ella.

JOSH: *Come up to the apartment if you can on your break for a kiss and squeeze.*

Ella responded right away.

ELLA: *No can do. I'm in a meeting with Sharon until four, but I could see you then.*

JOSH: *I'm in a meeting at four with the finance guys. How about we order dinner in at seven and call it a day in my apartment, so I can ravish you several times.*

ELLA: *I'll meet you up there at seven, ready to be ravished several times.*

I smiled and put my cell away, then found something else to do for the next hour until my meeting.

The rest of the afternoon went by quickly, and finally, seven o'clock rolled around. I checked my watch and packed up my laptop, cleaning off my desk before saying good night to my receptionist. I took the elevator up to the penthouse and was surprised to hear water running in the bathroom when I arrived.

I went into the bathroom, already unbuttoning my shirt, and saw that Ella was naked and bending over the bathtub, her back to me.

She was there and preparing to be ravished.

So, I ravished her.

LATER, WE SAT IN OUR BATHROBES AT THE DINING ROOM table and ate Chinese take-out by candlelight.

"So," Ella said and played with her chopsticks, trying to

pick up a shrimp but failing. "When are you going to tell me about your mysterious trip?"

"Oh, that," I said and sighed heavily, not sure I wanted to get into it at that moment. "Can we wait on that? I don't want to ruin the evening."

She didn't look happy at my request to delay discussing it. "It's that bad, is it? You're making me nervous."

"Don't be," I said and reached out to take her hand. "It just cuts close to the bone, that's all. I'd rather talk about something positive."

"Okay," she said, and then we moved on as easily as if she'd never even asked.

I was glad. I still felt this incredible sense of guilt about how I'd treated Penny -- callous and instrumental, treating her like she was a toy I enjoyed playing with rather than a person with a mind and heart of her own.

WE SLEPT IN LATE, DELIBERATELY TURNING OFF THE alarm so we didn't rush out and instead, took our time, enjoying a shower together, another round of lovemaking, and then breakfast together.

"So, what's up for you today? More meetings?"

"More meetings," I replied. "I sometimes wonder if I do anything else. What about you? More manuscripts?"

She laughed. "More manuscripts. I never wonder if I do anything else. I don't. That's all I do, and I love it."

"Do you really?" I asked, watching her while she poured herself a cup of coffee in her travel mug. "Don't you get sick of all the dreck?"

"It's great when you find something that holds your interest, that has an interesting voice. That makes the manuscripts that aren't quite up to snuff worth paging through."

"I'm glad you feel that way," I said. "It makes me feel better that we're getting good books."

"It's been my dream for several years, so nothing could make me happier than doing this for a living. Maybe I'd like to have a slush reader and me as the editor, but I know if I want to get there, I have to start here. I'm good."

We went to the elevator together and went down to our floors. When my floor came up, I bent down and gave her a warm kiss. "See you after work? I have a meeting over lunch with one of the IT guys."

"Sure," she said and waved at me as the doors closed.

I SPENT THE MORNING IN MEETINGS, AS I SAID, BUT THEN after a quick lunch at my desk, I met during the lunch hour with Jerome, one of the IT guys who did work for *The Chronicle*.

"What's up?" I asked as we sat at the boardroom table and were joined by conference call with another IT guy who was at the other building.

"We wanted to let you know about some hacking attempts on our server. We had a couple of phishing attempts recently, and we're afraid that one attempt was successful and one of the admins in personnel was hacked and the hacker gained access to our files."

"Damn," I said, not happy to hear that. "Who was it?"

"One of the newer staff who was tricked into changing her

password and who had her account hacked. The hacker gained access to our email server, unfortunately. We caught it that day, due to regular monitoring, but our server was compromised before we could get it secured. Everyone is being asked to create new passwords."

"Any idea who did this?"

Jerome shrugged. "Who can say? Our best guys are on it, but these hackers are pretty savvy. They know how to cover their tracks. We may never know. What we need to do is maybe train new employees better, so they don't get fooled by these phishing attempts."

"I'll talk to HR about an extra module on IT security."

We ended the meeting and I spent the next hour talking to my staff in HR about the data breach and what steps we could put in place to prevent it from happening again. Better training, in other words.

My only concern was who hacked us and why, but unfortunately, that was something we might never know.

For the next couple of days, I spent most of my time in the office, catching up on work and my nights with Ella. She never asked me again about my trip to Alabama and I never volunteered.

I hadn't heard anything from the rehab facility, so I assumed that things were going as expected. The intake worker I spoke with on the phone said that the first few days were the hardest as the addict went through withdrawal, although they did try to minimize the discomfort and for someone addicted to heroin or opiates, the facility used other medications such as methadone or buprenorphine.

Finally, I got a text from the manager of the facility that

Penny had passed through the first phase of detox and would be staying at the facility for the full six weeks of treatment.

I sent him an email thanking him for the update and that he should keep in touch, so I knew how Penny was doing. I wouldn't feel better until I knew she'd been successful.

I felt it was the least I could do.

17
ELLA

The next few days, I held off asking Josh about his trip to Millbrook, although I really wanted to know more about it. He'd tell me when he felt able, and I had to trust him to do so when the time was right. I realized it must have been something really personal for him to feel such deep guilt about it.

On Friday, in the morning just after I finished meeting with Sharon to review our week and talk about upcoming deadlines, I got a text from a number I didn't recognize. There was no name associated with the text, just a number.

.....*If you want to know more about the man you're currently sleeping with, you should follow this link.*

ELLA: *Who is this? If you don't identify yourself, I'll assume you're a troll or a hacker and I'll call IT.*

.....*You won't want to do that. Believe me, you'll want to know this about the man you're with. You don't really know anything about him and what he's done in the past. Ask him about his little trip to California. He was with her there. He's*

193

been fucking her for years. If you thought he stopped when he met you, you're wrong.

ELLA: *I already know about his trip so sorry, you're not going to get me to click on your link.*

.....You know about Penny? His little fucktoy?

That surprised me. Penny? I'd never heard Josh mention that name. He'd told me before about Christie and another girlfriend he had in college called Jennifer, but he'd never mentioned Penelope.

ELLA: *I know all about Penny. You're not telling me anything I don't already know.*

.....Then how can you continue to see him? He's cheating on you with her and you don't care?

ELLA: *Don't contact me again or I'll have the police find out who you are and charge you.*

......With what? Telling the truth?

I closed the text and deleted the number. Then, I blocked the number so whoever it was couldn't text me again.

But I kept the link.

I copied it and had it sitting on a document, just in case I decided I wanted to see it.

Did I want to see it?

Was it proof that Josh cheated on me with this woman, Penny? Had he been cheating on me with her all long?

I used my VPN and inserted the link in my browser. It didn't appear to be a suspect site according to my security software, so I clicked on it.

It took me to a website with several images of a woman -- a beautiful woman with long blonde hair, pretty, model-tall. She was smiling, and Josh was beside her, holding up a glass of beer. A younger Josh, and what looked like a very happy Josh.

Then another of them leaning in together, taken from behind, in a venue of some sort that appeared to be a club. Finally, one of him with his arm around her shoulder, with her leaning against the counter and him facing her, looking in her face. It appeared to be in a kitchen. I could make out a cupboard, and a sink, plus a window with lacy drapes. The date of the image was the weekend that Josh made the trip to his friend's funeral in Millbrook.

He must have been with her then.

Someone wanted to tell me that my boyfriend was cheating or had cheated on me with a girl called Penelope. Who could it have been? Was it a friend of theirs? Was it someone who knew me and was concerned about me?

Was it this Penny person herself?

I felt sick to my stomach and didn't know what to do with myself. I got up and cleaned my file cabinet out, reordering the files in a different alphabetical order. I rearranged the items on the top of my cabinet. I cleaned out my desk and changed the place where I kept my pens, pencils and other supplies.

I did everything I could not to think about Josh and this Penny woman the person messaged me about, but I couldn't escape the conclusion that Josh had cheated on me with Penny when he was in Millbrook.

He said he wasn't proud of something relating to Grant's death. Had he gone to the funeral and had sex after with this woman named Penelope?

I took out my cell and texted Steph.

ELLA: *I need your advice.*

A moment later, Steph responded.

STEPH: *Shoot. I'm all ears... (or in this case, eyes)*

ELLA: *You remember that Josh said he had something to*

tell me, but he wasn't ready yet to talk about it. He said it was something he wasn't proud of that had to do with his trip to go to the funeral of his old Army buddy, Grant.

STEPH: Yes, I remember. Did he get into a fight or something? Did he say something stupid at the memorial? Did he steal the mother's silverware? (Sorry, just trying to lighten the mood)

ELLA: Someone from a phone number I don't recognize just sent me a text claiming that Josh cheated on me with a woman named Penny. That she was his fucktoy. This person sent me a link with pics of Josh and this beautiful woman. One is dated a few days ago when Josh was at a funeral in Alabama.

STEPH: Oh, hun, I'm so sorry. Maybe Penny is an old girlfriend that he saw when he was at the funeral? Maybe it was all in the past?

ELLA: That was what I hoped was the case, but he said he felt guilt about something. Maybe he met her at the funeral and they had sex. Maybe he's guilty about it and is waiting to tell me about it when the right time comes.

STEPH: And what would that right time be?

ELLA: I have no idea. When he has enough balls to tell me?

STEPH: What would you think if he did tell you he cheated on you?

I didn't respond right away. What would I think? Of course, there was only one thing to do.

ELLA: I'd tell him to go fuck himself.

STEPH: Really?

ELLA: Yes. I was cheated on for years. Josh knew that. He was cheated on for years, too. How could he do it?

STEPH: Maybe it was when he was drunk and sad about his friend?

ELLA: That doesn't excuse it. Nope. If he did, we're through. Better I find out now than down the line when I think something more is going to happen between us.

STEPH: I guess you have to ask Josh. Get him to tell you about Penelope.

ELLA: *sigh* I hate confrontations. I try to avoid them at all costs. I'd rather send him an email and never see him again.

STEPH: You know you have to ask him now that you got that phone call and saw the pics. Just ask him. Say, "Tell me about Penny." Leave it at that. Let him expand. See if he admits he cheated.

ELLA: What if he says he hasn't seen her for years?

STEPH: Then, you have to tell him about the phone call and that you saw pics of them and see how he responds. The caller may be this Penny person who's jealous and is lying to get back at you or something.

ELLA: That's devious.

STEPH: Hun, I excel in recognizing and anticipating devious. I grew up with a sister who was devious as all get out and I had to learn to protect myself.

I remembered Steph talking about her sister when we first met in high school. Her older sister was a confirmed sociopath, who was a compulsive liar and thief who did terrible things and was finally sent to juvenile detention because of it. She moved away when Steph's mother and father finally had enough and cut her off. As far as I knew, Sheila was grifting somewhere in Boston, trying to find rich boyfriends to mooch off. She was beautiful and used her body to control men. She was so beautiful that men seemed to lose their minds with her and showered her with gifts and money. She clearly used them for their wealth.

Steph was worried that one day, Sheila would kill one of her men for insurance money.

ELLA: *I'll ask Josh. I'll have to work up the nerve first. I was so happy, Steph, and now this happens...*

STEPH: *The course of true love never did run smooth. Or so Willie Shakespeare says.*

ELLA: **sigh**

STEPH: *Ask him about Penny and let him tell you. You'll have to decide what to believe and whether to believe based on what he says. Sorry, kiddo. That's what you have to do.*

ELLA: *You're right. I'll ask him tomorrow.*

STEPH: *Let me know how it goes, and hun, I can come down there on the weekend if things don't work out the way you wish they would. Just let me know and I'll be there.*

ELLA: *Thanks. XOXOXO*

STEPH: *XOXOXO back at you.*

I put away my cell and sat at my desk, feeling especially glum.

I knew Steph was right. I had to confront Josh about this Penny woman and see what he said. I'd have a pretty good idea if he cheated on me by his answer. If he did, I just couldn't be with him. I couldn't tolerate a cheater, no matter the reason. I didn't care if he cheated on me because he was upset about the funeral. That wasn't good enough to justify sleeping with another woman.

No, sadly, if Josh cheated on me while he was away at the funeral, that was the end of our relationship. My stomach felt sick as I contemplated us breaking up. I couldn't imagine it.

The problem was, I didn't want to know. I didn't.

Josh and I were so good together. There was never a dull

moment, and the sex was off the charts. We both valued the same things and had the same goals.

It was Friday at lunch. I checked the Amtrak schedule -- a train was leaving at five thirty. I had enough time to get to my apartment, pack a bag, and then go to Concord.

I texted my mother.

ELLA: *Hey, Mom. I need to get away for the weekend. Is it okay if I come home? Just until Sunday night? I won't be home until one in the morning so don't wait up.*

MOM: *Nonsense. I'll be there to pick you up. I don't want you taking a taxi home at that hour.*

ELLA: *No seriously. I'll be fine. I've been living in Manhattan and can take care of myself. Go to bed. You know you're useless after ten at night.*

MOM: *If you say so... I don't like it though. If you change your mind, I can come and meet you at the bus station.*

ELLA: *No, really. See you in the morning, okay?*

MOM: *Okay. You do know that your father is in Washington for a meeting.*

ELLA: *I know he's away.*

MOM: *Is there something wrong, dear? This is kind of out of the blue.*

ELLA: *It's good actually. I just need to get away from the bustle of the city for a few days.*

Then, I thought better of it.

ELLA: *Oh, hell. Yes, something's wrong. Someone told me that Josh cheated on me with an old girlfriend. Or maybe he never stopped seeing her. I don't know which. Regardless, I saw pics of him with her a week ago when he was at the funeral of his friend from the Army.*

MOM: *Did you ask him about it?*

ELLA: *What's he going to say? Yes?*

MOM: *He might say no. That your source was wrong.*

ELLA: *The pics don't lie. I will talk to him about it, but now, I need some time away to get my mind straight.*

MOM: *Oh, dear. It sounds like you're in far deeper than I suspected. You really care about Josh.*

ELLA: *I thought I did. I thought he cared about me, but if this is true, I guess I should swear off men altogether.*

MOM: *Oh, sweetheart, no. Don't say that. You just have to find the right man. You will. Give it time.*

ELLA: *Whatever. I have to go back to my apartment and get ready. See you in the morning.*

MOM: *I love you, Ellie.*

ELLA: *Love you back.*

I sent Sharon an email saying I'd developed a crushing migraine and needed to take the rest of the day off. She was fine with it and hoped I felt better. I knew she'd be generous and let me leave early.

I debated whether to call Reg and ask him to take me home, but I just didn't want to risk running into Josh. I didn't want to have to see or talk to anyone. I just wanted to go somewhere and be completely alone.

So, I left the building and didn't bother to call Reg for the car. I certainly didn't tell Josh. I didn't want to have to confront him about this Penelope woman.

How could he do it to me, knowing what I'd gone through?

I LEFT THE BUILDING THROUGH THE BACK ENTRANCE AND walked to the subway, then made my way to my apartment in Chelsea. When I got inside, I quickly packed an overnight bag with enough clothes and personal effects to take me through to Sunday night. I grabbed my laptop and case and left, taking the subway to Penn Station.

I felt a heavy weight of sadness descend over me as I waited for the train. I could have confronted Josh, gone to his office and demanded he tell me about Penny, but all I really wanted to do was cry.

I wasn't going to do that.

I was *not* going to cry over Josh. Instead, I'd go away for a few days and get my head clear.

THE TRIP FROM NEW YORK TO BOSTON TOOK FOUR AND A half hours. It was more than enough time for me to worry that I'd made a mistake and shouldn't have run off so quickly. I wasn't going to change course and go back. I told myself that it would be a nice break from the daily routine. I told myself that I could get away from everything for a couple of days, recharge and the go back and face Josh and learn the truth about Penny.

Whoever she was and whatever Josh did with her. It made me sick to even consider him with another woman. Not because of the sex, but because of the betrayal. He'd been betrayed by Christie. I'd been betrayed by Derek.

How could he do that to me?

If he had, I was completely and totally wrong about him.

I realized I had grown far too attached to Josh far too quickly. It was a mistake to let myself fall so easily. I didn't really know him very well, after all.

Of course, he sent me a text asking where I was.

JOSH: Hey, where are you? I popped down to see you and Sharon said you'd gone home with a migraine. Hope you're feeling better, but you really should have told Reg you were leaving. I don't like the thought of you going around on your own until we know who Mr. Fedora really is.

I didn't answer right away but then I realized he'd text me and pester me until I did.

ELLA: I have a really bad migraine. I told you that I get them now and then. They can last a couple of days, so I'm sorry if we have to cancel plans to spend the weekend together. I'll let you know when the migraine lifts. Sorry about this.

JOSH: Don't apologize for something you can't control. Can I come by and look after you? I could bring chicken soup or ice cream, or whatever makes you feel better when you get a migraine. Coffee? Chocolate? Or are those triggers? I can't remember.

ELLA: No, just time and my meds make it better. I'll let you know.

JOSH: Okay. Miss you.

ELLA: Me, too.

I didn't send my usual response filled with XOXOXOs.

I just couldn't do it.

THE BUS ARRIVED A HALF HOUR AFTER MIDNIGHT AND I was one of a dozen people on the bus from Boston. I was exceptionally tired and sad when I got off the bus and wasn't at all surprised to see my mother waiting beside her car.

"Mom, I told you not to," I said, and we hugged. She was wearing a coat over her pajamas and didn't seem to care.

"I couldn't let you take a cab home so late at night. I don't care what you said. Now, get in and let's get you home."

We drove up to the house and my mom parked the car in

the circular driveway. I got out and stood in front of the house I grew up in and breathed in the fresh night air. It smelled a lot different in Concord than in Manhattan.

Of course, I associated that smell with meeting and falling for Josh, and it brought back a wave of sadness that things had fallen apart so quickly after being so promising.

"Come on dear," my mother said, as if sensing my sadness. "Let's get you into your PJs and into your bed."

I let her put her arm around me and lead me inside, glad for the comfort.

Later, after changing into my pajamas, I laid in my bed and she kissed me on the cheek.

"Whatever happened today, it will look better in the morning. Good night, dear."

"Good night mom," I said.

My cell dinged, and I knew it was Josh, so I turned my cell off completely. Then, I turned over, closing my eyes, knowing that sleep would be a long time in coming.

18
JOSH

I read over Ella's text and something didn't feel quite right about it.

I remembered that she said she sometimes got headaches, especially when she didn't get enough sleep or was under stress. We'd been staying up late and sometimes waking up to have sex in the middle of the night. Was I running her ragged?

I just couldn't get enough of her and she seemed to feel the same way, responsive to my every touch and kiss.

I thought of her lying alone in her apartment's Murphy bed and felt bad, but I needed to give her the space to get over the migraine if she asked for it. My instinct was to go and stay with her, or better yet, have her come and stay at the apartment with me for the weekend so I could look after her, but I didn't want to argue with her when she was in pain.

It did upset me that she left the building and went home without telling Reg. I decided to talk to him and maybe have someone go there and make sure the place was covered. We still had no idea who Mr. Fedora was, and I didn't want to risk anything just in case it was one of my former staff members who was terminated and who wanted to hurt me and mine.

I left my office and went down to the security office. I glanced up at the camera and pressed the button on the security door. The duty officer buzzed me inside. Reg was in his office, reading over some report.

"Mr. Macintyre. What can I do for you?"

"Ella left the building without letting us know," I said when I sat in the chair across from his desk.

He frowned. "When?"

"I don't know for sure but probably after lunch. Let me check."

I texted Sharon.

JOSH: *When did Ella go home with her migraine?*

SHARON: *She messaged me just after lunch. I suppose it would be soon after. Is something wrong? Didn't she tell you?*

JOSH: *No, she did. I was just wondering what time she left.*

I then decided to tell Sharon about Mr. Fedora.

JOSH: *I'll be right up. I need to talk to you about something.*

SHARON: *I'm here at your disposal.*

I turned to Reg. "She probably left just after lunch hour, but I don't have an exact time."

Reg left the office and went to the videos in the control room. "I'll check the feed and see when she left, check to see if Mr. Fedora wasn't in sight but I'm pretty sure we would have caught him if he was."

"Good. And make sure to send someone to her place to watch over, just in case."

"Will do."

Then, I went up to Sharon's office and when I arrived, I closed the door behind me and sat across from her.

"What's up, boss? Is there an issue with Ella?"

I shook my head. "No, not at all. I've been followed recently by someone we can't identify and so we don't know who it is or what his motives are. I hired a security company to watch over the building and ghost both Ella and me when we leave and when Ella goes to her place, just to be safe."

She frowned. "Oh, I'm sorry to hear that. Who do you think it is?"

"I honestly have no idea."

"Do you have any enemies?"

I shrugged. "Could be a disgruntled former employee. Could be a business competitor who is doing research on me. Until we have more information, I have no way of knowing, but I want to be safe rather than sorry, on the off-chance it's a nutcase."

"That's a scary thought. But given the employment related shootings that happen every year, I guess you have to be careful."

"Precisely my thoughts," I replied. "Anyway, Ella knows about it and has agreed to be careful to let the security people know when she's coming and going so they can ghost her, but she didn't when she left the building today. I know she's not feeling well so it just might be an oversight on her part. Sometimes people with migraines get a kind of brain fog and she forgot to let security know. Whatever the case, I have someone going over to make sure her building is watched for the weekend."

"That must be expensive," Sharon said.

"If it protects me or Ella, it's worth every penny."

We spoke a few moments longer about Ella and then I left, feeling somewhat better that Ella had just forgotten about security because of her migraine. At least Sharon knew now and would be aware in case anything came up in the future.

I had a late meeting to get through, but I wanted to text Ella and make sure she was okay and didn't need anything.

JOSH: Hey, sorry to bother you when you're not feeling well, but did you know you forgot to let Reg know you were leaving? I realize you probably forgot because of the migraine but don't worry. I'll send someone over to watch the apartment for the weekend. If you need anything, let me know and I'll come right over. Anything at all -- coffee, takeout food, me naked and wearing a manservant apron -- anything.

I didn't hear back from her and at first I put it down to her not checking her cell because she wasn't feeling well but when she hadn't responded by nine that night, I started to panic.

I called Reg.

"Any news on Ella's place? I've texted her and she didn't respond."

Reg put me on hold for a moment to check with his man on the street watching Ella's apartment.

"My guy Parker said there's been no movement since he's been watching. There's a light on, but he hasn't seen her come or go."

"Okay, thanks. She usually gets back to me quickly, so I was a bit worried."

"Do you want Parker to go up and check on her?"

"No, no, that's okay. I'll drop by and bring her some food or something just to check on her."

"Okay. I'll tell Parker we'll be by. I'll be outside waiting in the car."

I ended the call and sat in the quiet of my apartment, wondering if she was just sleeping.

JOSH: Hey, I'm coming by with some hot soup that I hear is excellent for people who are sick or under the weather. I'll be by in twenty minutes.

She didn't reply, so Reg drove me to the Pho restaurant and waited while I got a takeout container of the spicy noodle soup that Ella loved. Reg took me to her place and we drove alongside Parker, who was sitting in a car across from Ella's building.

"Josh will run up and check on Ella," Reg said to Parker.

We parked, and I grabbed the Pho and went to the front entrance. Ella had given me a key, so I let myself into the building and took the stairs to her third-floor apartment. I went inside, but she wasn't there. I checked the bathroom, but the place was empty.

I panicked.

JOSH: Where are you? I'm at your place and you're not here.

Nothing.

I ran down the stairs to the car and got inside. "She's not home."

"What?" Reg frowned. "Parker said she didn't leave the place. He can see the entrance from here -- both the front and rear exits are visible.

I glanced over to the building and sure enough, you could see through the entrance to the rear door. The entry was well-lit and there was no way Parker could miss someone going out either exit.

She wasn't at home.

I texted her right away.

JOSH: Ella, please let me know where you are. I'm worried because of Mr. Fedora. Text me as soon as you get this.

I waited.

"She's not responding to my texts," I said.

"Did you two have a fight or something? Any reason she might not want to talk to you?"

I frowned.

"Not that I know of."

"Is it possible she's out shopping?"

"She went home with a migraine headache."

Reg nodded. "Would she go to the ER because of it? Sometimes, people with migraines get a shot of painkiller."

"She said she had medication for it and just needed to sleep."

"Maybe you should call the police and report her missing."

I took my cell out once more but there still wasn't an answer.

JOSH: Ella, I'm going to call the police and report you missing, so if you get this in the next thirty minutes, please let me know that you're okay and I won't. Otherwise, I'm going to file a missing person's report.

"I just messaged her and told her I was going to file a missing person's report on her if I don't hear back in half an hour. Just in case she's not answering for a reason but is fine."

"Good idea," Reg said.

We sat in the car and talked about Mr. Fedora and what was being done to identify him.

"I sent his photo to a friend I have who works in the FBI and asked him to pass it through their facial recognition software. At least we'll know if he had an FBI or police file on him."

"That's good," I said. "I need to know who he is. That's the only way we'll know if he's a threat."

"It won't take him long to identify the guy if he's in the system."

"When do you think we'll know?"

Reg shrugged. "Should have something back tomorrow night."

"Thanks," I said and checked my watch. "Time's up. If she hasn't responded, I'm going to file a report."

I checked my cell.

ELLA: I'm fine. I came home for the weekend. I'm in Concord at my parent's place. I'll be back on Sunday night. I'm sorry you went to so much trouble to find me.

I frowned.

JOSH: Why didn't you message me? I would have taken you to the train.

ELLA: I needed to be alone. We can talk about it when I get back.

JOSH: Talk about what? Tell me what's the matter.

ELLA: Josh, I'm not feeling well, and don't want to talk about this right now.

JOSH: Of course. But seriously, Ella. I was so worried about you. I was afraid Mr. Fedora had abducted you or harmed you in some way. You can't imagine the thoughts that went through my head.

ELLA: I'm fine. I'm sorry I made you worry so much, but I didn't think you'd find out I wasn't at home.

JOSH: You have to know I'd be worried about you when I learned you weren't feeling well and had a bad migraine. I wanted to come over and look after you.

211

ELLA: I just needed to be alone and didn't think you'd be so concerned.

JOSH: Can I come and see you in Concord? I'll drive up. It won't take me too long.

ELLA: No, Josh. We can talk when I get back, okay? Just give me the weekend and I promise we'll talk when I get back.

JOSH: Okay. I don't think we should wait, but I will if you really want.

ELLA: I do. I'll let you know when I get back.

JOSH: Please let me know what time your train is going to be in and I'll pick you up.

ELLA: Okay.

JOSH: I'll see you Sunday. I miss you.

ELLA: See you Sunday.

She didn't respond in the usual way, with XOXO and echoing my sentiments so I knew something was wrong.

"She's fine. She's at her parent's place in Concord," I said to Reg.

He shook his head. "She should have let someone know she was going out of town."

"She wasn't thinking clearly," I said, not wanting to get into the whole business. "You can take me back to the building. I'm going to drive to Concord tonight and stay there for the rest of the weekend."

"Do you want me to take you?"

"No, but you could trail me for a while to make sure I'm not being followed."

"Okay."

Reg took me back to the building where I packed an overnight bag and grabbed my laptop. Then, I left the apartment. I programmed in Concord's Marriott and drove off, with

Reg following me for the first twenty miles until I was on the outskirts of the Bronx. He flashed his lights at me and then turned back towards Manhattan.

I didn't know what was wrong with Ella, but something was definitely up. I couldn't imagine it was merely the migraine stopping her from notifying security, not responding to my texts, and then returning to Concord without telling me or anyone.

Whatever it was, I was sure it had to do with our relationship.

I felt exhausted after a long day at work and my worry about Ella, but at the same time, I needed to drive to Concord and talk to her.

I didn't want to wait.

19
ELLA

I slept late, not waking until eleven in the morning. I crept out of bed then I pulled on my robe and slippers and padded out to the kitchen, where my mother was sitting at the kitchen island reading the morning paper, a coffee mug in hand.

"Good morning, sleepy head," she said and smiled. "Feeling better?"

"Yes," I said and went to the coffee maker to pour myself a cup.

"Are you going to tell me what's wrong, so I can help you?"

I poured some cream in my coffee and stirred, delaying my response because I wasn't sure I wanted to tell her about Josh.

"Come on," she said and came over, slipping her arm around my shoulder. "You can tell me. What did he do to upset you? Did you two have a lover's quarrel?"

"No," I said, and it was then I felt my eyes tear up for the first time. "He cheated on me."

Then I broke down and covered my eyes. My mother pulled me into her arms and rocked me back and forth.

"Oh, my poor girl," she said and stroked my hair. "There'll be another man come along before you know it."

"Not like Josh," I said, and wiped my eyes. "I thought everything was so perfect between us."

"Tell me what happened."

We sat at the island and I told her about the messages I got and the link to the page with pictures of Josh and this blonde woman.

"One of the pictures was dated the weekend Josh went away. The day of his friend's funeral. The messages said Josh had been cheating on me with her the whole time."

"Did you ask him about it?"

I frowned. "No, I just left. I needed to get away and think things through."

My mother sighed. "It seems to me that you have to ask Josh before you do anything. Maybe the person who sent the messages was lying. You didn't even give Josh a chance."

"If he cheated on me, he doesn't deserve a chance."

"*If* is the proper word. You don't know. You only have some anonymous person's word and a picture. Was it of them having sex?"

"No," I said and frowned. "It was a picture of them in a kitchen and he had his hands on her shoulders."

"Maybe he was just talking to her."

"But there were other pictures of them together, and they were clearly romantically involved."

She didn't say anything for a moment and then I heard her sigh.

"Sweetheart, you were hurt badly by Derek. I understand

it's made it hard to trust another man, but you have to give Josh the chance to explain before you rush to judgement. Not all men are like Derek."

"I didn't think Josh was like him, but if he was cheating the whole time we were seeing each other..."

"You don't know that for a fact. Talk to Josh. Let him explain. If he admits he was cheating or can't explain that picture of him with the blonde, then tell him it's over."

I nodded. I knew she was right. I hadn't given Josh a chance to explain because I was too afraid of what he'd say. I didn't want to hear him give me some lame excuse about being heartbroken over his friend's death and falling into this woman's arms for comfort. I didn't want to hear him say he was just drunk and didn't really mean to do it.

My mother reached out and took my hand, squeezing. She gave me a soft smile of encouragement.

"Call Josh, or text him, whatever it is you young people do. Give him a chance. If he's been good to you up till now, he deserves at least a chance to explain."

"Okay."

I got up from the counter and went to the bathroom for a quick shower. The spray of hot water always seemed to help me get my head on straight.

ONCE I WAS DRESSED AND HAD A FRESH CUP OF COFFEE, I sat at the dining room table and took out my laptop. On my messenger was notice of five messages.

I figured they were all from Josh, and when I clicked on the icon, I was right.

The latest message was from thirty minutes earlier.

I read over the messages in order of their timestamp.

JOSH: ELLA, I'M COMING TO CONCORD. I'LL BE STAYING AT *the Marriott. Please message or call me so we can talk.*

JOSH: *I'm just passing Boston. I stopped at a gas station and wanted to let you know that you matter more to me than anything and I need to know what I've done to make you leave.*

JOSH: *I've checked in to the hotel and am lying on the bed, feeling lost without you. Please, tell me what's wrong.*

JOSH: *It's morning. I barely slept. Please, Ella. Talk to me.*

HE SOUNDED SO UPSET THAT I'D LEFT AND WASN'T talking to him.

ELLA: COME OVER TO MY HOUSE. MY MOM'S GONE OUT FOR *a while. We can talk.*

THEN I WAITED. JOSH ARRIVED ABOUT FIFTEEN MINUTES later, and his face was pale, his eyes haggard.

"Come in," I said and led him inside to the living room.

He came over to me and I knew he wanted to hug me, but I quickly sat on the chair facing the sofa.

He sat across from me, clearly dejected.

"Tell me what's the matter, Ella."

I took in a deep breath, because it was now or never. I had to ask him and he had to tell me.

"The other day, you said you had something to talk to me about that you weren't proud of. I want you to tell me now."

He sighed and leaned forward, his elbows on his knees, his hands clasped. He didn't meet my eyes. "My army buddy Grant killed himself."

"I know," I replied and while my instinct would have been to reach out to squeeze his hand to comfort him, I didn't. "You already told me that much."

"He had a younger sister," Josh said and a wave of adrenaline coursed through me. I tried to prepare myself for what he was going to say.

He cheated on me with her.

"You slept with her while you were at the funeral," I blurted out.

His face blanched and he glanced up at me, frowning.

"No, *no*," he said and grabbed my hand. "I would never sleep with someone else. Why would you think that? How could you even imagine I'd consider sleeping with someone else?"

I shrugged, my eyes burning. "We were both cheated on," I said, my voice breaking. "Both of us should be more than able to consider it. I figured you're just as likely as anyone to cheat."

"I never cheated on you. I want you," he said knelt beside my chair, my hands in his. "Only you."

"Then what happened that you could be so guilty about?"

He exhaled and glanced away.

"Before I met Christie, when I was in the Army, I used to sleep with Grant's sister when we were in the States on leave."

I nodded, waiting for the rest of the story.

"I thought she was fine with it. You know, we both were young and single and not into long-term relationships. I thought she really meant it when she said no strings attached, but apparently, she thought it meant more. She thought that because we kept getting together each time I was in the States, that I couldn't live without her. She thought we'd take the next step and get engaged, and then marry. She imagined that we'd move to Manhattan and she'd be my wife. Of course, I had no interest in her besides a fun sex partner now and then. I *used* her, Ella. Crassly. Unthinkingly. I used her and then I forgot about her when I met Christie once I was back home and out of the service. Christie and I got engaged and I guess Penny crashed when she learned about it in the papers."

"She was wrong to expect more than you offered," I said.

"*I* was wrong to use her like that, not seeing that she was getting in deeper than I was. That she was expecting more. We kept our relationship secret because we were both afraid that Grant would be angry and disapprove of it. It made it easy to see it as nothing important -- at least for me. It wasn't public, so it didn't matter. I was callous, not realizing she felt differently."

"What happened at the funeral? She was there. Did you have a big scene or something?"

He nodded. "She was drunk and high as well. She started using heavier drugs after we stopped seeing each other. She went downhill and became depressed. She's an addict, Ella," he said, his voice impassioned. "Heroin. Meth. She lives in this dump of a rooming house and has tracks up her arms. She prostitutes herself for money for her drugs. It caused a real divide in the family and they pretty much disowned her. Grant's suicide sent her off the deep end, and I was there to see her hit rock bottom."

I nodded and waited for the rest. "And then what?"

"I gave her money, because she was clearly hurting. She

started to hit me up for more and more. Finally, I said that unless she got help, I'd turn off the tap. I paid for a bed at a rehab facility in California and she agreed to go. That's why I was there. I picked her up in Millbrook and flew her to the facility near LA. Since I was there, I stayed with David."

"That's where you went," I said and felt a surge of hope in me. "This was the big secret you were keeping from me? You paid for her rehab and took her there?"

He nodded. "We never slept together. I never kissed her. I just paid for her rehab and took her there."

I shook my head, ashamed that I'd been so wrong.

"That's nothing to be ashamed of. It's noble."

"I was horrible to her," he said and shook his head. "I treated her like an object to use when I felt like it. To forget about when I found something I liked better. No wonder she crashed."

I leaned over and kissed him softly. "You didn't mislead her. She misled herself. Josh, you can't take responsibility for the whole world on your shoulders. She's responsible for her own issues, not you. There must be something in their family -- mental illness, abuse, neglect -- something that led Penny to do drugs. People who abuse drugs are self-medicating. They need help and the drugs take the pain away for a while. It's not your fault."

"I wish I could believe you, but if I hadn't led her on..."

"Did you promise her to love her and only her? To stay with her till death do you part? If not, you didn't lead her on."

"But I was so heartless. I didn't see how her idea about what we meant to each other changed. I didn't read the signs. I was selfish and self-absorbed. Then, when I met Christie, I just moved on without a thought."

I felt tears well up in my eyes. I'd been so wrong about him...

"I have a confession to make, too," I said and got up, pulling him over to the sofa. I sat, and he sat down beside me.

"What?"

I told him about the anonymous messages I received and the page of pictures of him and Penny.

"Oh, God, I'm so sorry," he said, frowning. "If I'd told you right away about Penny, you would have known that those pictures meant nothing. This is my fault. I should have come clean, but I just felt so bad overall."

"We both should have been more open," I said and reached over to cup his face. "I'm sorry I didn't just ask you outright, but I was afraid that I'd been betrayed again."

"I would never cheat on you," he said. "Never. I love you, Ella. I'm in love with you. I have been since that day in the elevator."

"That's crazy," I said, my eyes filled with tears.

"It's true," he said and laughed, his own eyes misty. "I love you, Ella. Don't run away from me again. You can always ask me anything and I'll always tell you the truth. I don't want to ever be apart from you again."

"I'm so sorry I doubted you." We kissed and embraced, and I felt a wave of relief flood through my body, my heart feeling like it could burst with happiness. "I love you, Josh. I can't imagine not having you in my life. This past day has been utter hell because I thought we'd have to end it."

We kissed again, our arms tight around each other.

That was how my mother found us as she came in the front door. Our kiss ended, and I glanced over only to see her raise her eyebrows and quickly turn around and go back outside.

"Mom, it's okay," I called out. "You can come back in."

She did come back in, her face flushed bright pink. "Whew!" she said and fanned herself. "I thought you two were having a moment and didn't want to interrupt."

"We were having a moment, but it's all good." I stood and pulled Josh up. "Mom, this is Josh Macintyre."

Josh held his hand out. "So happy to finally meet you, Mrs. Carlson. You should know that I'm in love with your daughter and I just told her I didn't want us to ever be apart again."

Of course, my mother was ecstatic to meet Josh and of most especially, to hear his declaration of love.

"Oh, you're going to have me in tears with that kind of talk. Come here and give me a big old hug," she said, and he laughed when she embraced him, not seeming to mind her overly affectionate nature, embracing her back and smiling at me.

Josh and my mother hugged for a moment and then he pulled back, his hands on her arms. "I'm a bit worried to meet your husband, though. Is he not home?"

"He's in Washington for the weekend."

"Do you think he'll forgive me for my father's past indiscretions?"

"There's nothing to forgive," my mother said and waved her hand dismissively. "When you two finally meet, all he'll care about is whether you've made our little girl happy."

Josh turned to me and smiled softly. "That's all that matters to me."

He took my hand and squeezed, and it was then I finally knew that everything was going to be all right.

20

JOSH

E PILOGUE
       While Ella packed her bag, I sat at the kitchen island and spoke with Mrs. Carlson.

"What advice do you have for me in dealing with Governor Carlson?" I asked, sipping the fresh cup of coffee she made for me. She'd invited me back to Concord at Christmas so I could meet the Governor.

"Be forthright and honest," Mrs. Carlson said. "He doesn't have time for games and doesn't tolerate them in others. If you do that, you should be fine with him. He's sometimes blunt -- brutally blunt -- but he doesn't lie so you always know where you stand with him."

"That's a good trait to have. I admire honesty."

She smiled. "Then you two should get along fine."

Ella came out of the bedroom, her overnight bag in hand.

"Sorry to leave but Josh wanted us to go to his house in Montauk. The weather's good this weekend and it's probably one of the last nice weekends we'll get until spring."

"Don't you worry about it," Mrs. Carlson said. "You two go and enjoy the weather. I'm all booked up with bridge and a girl's night out tonight, so I'll be fine."

While Ella and her mom kissed and hugged each other, I carried Ella's bag out to the car.

"Nice to meet you," I said to Mrs. Carlson and gave her a hug. She kissed my cheek and then wiped it off.

"So good to meet you, Josh. You come up for Christmas and spend some time with us. I'll make sure Ella's father is on his best behavior."

"I look forward to it."

Then, we drove off, back down the coast to Montauk to spend the rest of the weekend at the house.

THE HOUSE HAD BEEN EMPTY FOR MONTHS, AND IT smelled a bit stale, so I opened the patio doors leading onto the deck. The wind off the ocean brought in the fresh salty air, the lace curtains billowing around me. Down below, a hundred feet away, I could hear the waves crash against the surf.

"My God, Josh, this house is amazing."

Ella stood beside me and I heard her take in a deep breath. She had her eyes closed, clearly enjoying the smell of the salt air.

"The house is beautiful, but if I was here by myself, I'd be unhappy. There are so many memories here for me of my mother and father. You're so lucky you still have both of them."

"I know," she said and took my hand. "I am lucky."

We spent the last few hours of sunlight walking the beach, hand in hand. Then, we went inside and spent some time getting our meal ready. We'd stopped in town on the way to the house to pick up some food and planned on grilling some steaks. While I seasoned the meat, Ella made a fresh salad and slipped a loaf of French Bread in the oven.

"This kitchen is a cook's fantasy," she said and ran her fingers along the countertop. "The refrigerator, the range, the sinks..."

"My mother loved to cook. We could have had a chef, but we only did for special occasions. The rest of the time, my mother spent planning and preparing our meals. She should have been a caterer, she enjoyed it so much. So, my father made sure to build her the very best kitchen possible."

"He must have loved her," she said and smiled.

"He did," I said, remembering my father's words in his letter to us boys.

My one piece of advice on how to have a happy life? Marry well. Have a family with many children. Love your family with all your heart, the way I did you and your mother.

I watched Ella as she ripped up lettuce and chopped vegetables for the salad. I knew at that moment, that she belonged in my mother's kitchen, using it the way my mother would have wanted.

I went to her and slipped my arms around her waist, pulling her against me.

"This is nice," I said and kissed her neck.

"It is."

She turned around in my arms and we kissed deeply.

"Things turned out much better than I expected," she said when the kiss ended. "I figured I'd be crying my eyes out in Concord, my mother consoling me with hot cocoa and cheesecake."

"Does cheesecake console you?"

"No, but it does console my mother. I'm a crème brûlée kind of gal."

"That's right. I'll have to remember that for when you need consoling in the future."

We hugged each other and then the timer on the stove went off. The grill was ready for the steaks.

We ate at the dining room table only because it was a bit too windy on the patio, but we had a nice view of the ocean as the stars began to rise.

LATER, WHILE ELLA SAT READING THE PAPER, I MOVED our bags to the master bedroom that my parents used to share. I hadn't been there since the early summer, when my father asked me to come out and retrieve some of my mother's pictures for him. He was too sick to make the trip.

While I was standing at the large dresser my mother used, I saw her jewelry box and opened it, wondering what was still there. My father had refused to pack up her things when she died and instead, kept everything on the dresser as she left it.

There, on the top shelf of the jewelry box, was her engagement ring, the single solitary diamond huge in a wide platinum band. She had been so thin at the end that she couldn't wear it any longer and so she'd taken to wearing only her wedding band on a necklace around her neck. She hoped that one day, one of us boys would give her engagement ring to our bride-to-be.

I hadn't given it to Christie, for she had already picked out her engagement ring -- a huge square diamond surrounded by emeralds.

When I saw the ring sitting there, waiting, I knew what I wanted to do.

I picked it up and slipped it into the pocket in my sweater. Then, I went out onto the patio where Ella, brave soul that she was, was sitting on the huge sectional, her head back, watching the stars overhead.

She smiled when she saw me and patted the sofa beside her.

"Come and sit with me," she said. "The wind has died down and stars are so beautiful, and you can see so many out here. I could live here and be quite happy."

Instead, I knelt beside her and took her hand.

"Ella," I said and reached into my pocket, removing the ring. "This was my mother's engagement ring. She wanted one of her sons to give it to their fiancée one day and I hope I can fulfill her wish. I love you and I want you to be my wife. Will you marry me?"

She covered her mouth and glanced down at the ring. "Josh..." She let me slip the ring on her finger and it almost fit perfectly. "It's so beautiful." She stared at the ring, and I feared she'd say no.

"This is sudden," she said softly, glancing up at me, her expression serious. "We've only been dating for a few months."

"I know, but I can't deny how I feel. If this weekend taught me anything, it's that I love you and can't imagine life without you."

"I can't either," she said. " Of course, I'll marry you. I love you and can't imagine life without you."

We kissed and spent the rest of the evening lying on the sofa, a blanket wrapped around us, watching the stars of the Milky Way rise in the sky overhead.

. . .

THE END OF BOOK TWO

BOOK THREE: TAME ME AVAILABLE NOW!

ABOUT THE AUTHOR

S. E. Lund writes erotic, contemporary, new adult and paranormal romance. She lives with her family of humans and animals in Beautiful British Columbia Canada on the side of a mountain and in sight of an active volcano. She dreams of living in a warm climate where snow is just a word in a dictionary.

For More Information:
www.selund.net
selund2012@gmail.com

ALSO BY S. E. LUND

THE UNRESTRAINED SERIES:

THE AGREEMENT: Book 1 in the Unrestrained Series

THE COMMITMENT: Book 2 in the Unrestrained Series

UNRESTRAINED: Book 3 in the Unrestrained Series

UNBREAKABLE: Book 4 in the Unrestrained Series

FOREVER AFTER: Book 5 in the Unrestrained Series

EVERLASTING: Book 6 in the Unrestrained Series

DRAKE FOREVER: Book 7 in the Unrestrained Series

ENDLESS: Book 8 in the Unrestrained Series (Dec 17 2018)

THE UNRESTRAINED SERIES COLLECTION ONE
(BOOKS 1 - 3)

THE DRAKE SERIES:

DRAKE RESTRAINED: Book 1 in the Drake Series

DRAKE UNWOUND: Book 2 in the Drake Series

DRAKE UNBOUND: Book 3 in the Drake Series

THE MACINTYRE BROTHERS SERIES

Tempt Me: Book One

Tease Me: Book Two

Tame Me: Book Three (2019)

STANDALONE BOOKS:

MR. BIG SHOT

MATCHED

IF YOU FALL

THE BAD BOY SERIES:

BAD BOY SAINT: Book 1 in the Bad Boy Series

BAD BOY SINNER: Book 2 in the Bad Boy Series

BAD BOY SOLDIER: Book 3 in the Bad Boy Series

BAD BOY SAVIOR: Book 4 in the Bad Boy Series

THE BAD BOY SERIES COLLECTION: All 4 books together in one volume.

PARANORMAL ROMANCE SERIES:

DOMINION: BOOK 1

ASCENSION: BOOK 2

RETRIBUTION: BOOK 3

RESURRECTION: BOOK 4

REDEMPTION: BOOK 5

THE DOMINION SERIES COMPLETE COLLECTION

www.ingramcontent.com/pod-product-compliance
Lightning Source LLC
Chambersburg PA
CBHW020105180626
46812CB00006B/2476